*The Great Brain
Reforms*

OTHER YEARLING BOOKS YOU WILL ENJOY:

MORE ADVENTURES OF THE GREAT BRAIN, *John D. Fitzgerald*

ME AND MY LITTLE BRAIN, *John D. Fitzgerald*

THE GREAT BRAIN AT THE ACADEMY, *John D. Fitzgerald*

THE GREAT BRAIN, *John D. Fitzgerald*

THE RETURN OF THE GREAT BRAIN, *John D. Fitzgerald*

THE GREAT BRAIN DOES IT AGAIN, *John D. Fitzgerald*

TALES OF A FOURTH GRADE NOTHING, *Judy Blume*

SUPERFUDGE, *Judy Blume*

FRECKLE JUICE, *Judy Blume*

THE ONE IN THE MIDDLE IS THE GREEN KANGAROO,
Judy Blume

YEARLING BOOKS are designed especially to entertain and enlighten young people. Charles F. Reasoner, Professor Emeritus of Children's Literature and Reading, New York University is consultant to this series.

For a complete listing of all Yearling titles, write to Dell Publishing Co., Inc., Promotion Department, P.O. Box 3000, Pine Brook, N.J. 07058.

The Great Brain Reforms

ILLUSTRATED BY MERCER MAYER

by John D. Fitzgerald

A YEARLING BOOK

Published by
Dell Publishing Co., Inc.
1 Dag Hammarskjold Plaza
New York, New York 10017
Text copyright © 1973 by John D. Fitzgerald
Illustrations copyright © 1973 by The Dial Press
All rights reserved. No part of this book may be reproduced in
any form or by any means without the prior written permission of
The Dial Press, excepting brief quotes used in connection with
reviews written specifically for inclusion in a magazine or newspaper.
For information address The Dial Press, New York, New York 10017.
Yearling ® TM 913705, Dell Publishing Co., Inc.
ISBN: 0-440-44841-1
Reprinted by arrangement with The Dial Press
Printed in the United States of America
Eighteenth Dell printing—August 1984

CW

For Ruth and Gerald

Contents

*The Great Brain
Reforms*

CHAPTER ONE

The Return Home

MY BROTHER TOM and eldest brother Sweyn arrived home for summer vacation on Sunday, June 5, 1898. I remember the date very well because, just two weeks later, the entire town of Park City was destroyed by the worst fire in the history of Utah. My brothers had been attending the Catholic Academy for Boys in Salt Lake City. We only had a one-room schoolhouse in Adenville where Mr. Standish taught the first through the sixth grades. I had just finished the fourth grade and wouldn't be going away to the academy for two years.

Tom kept looking around when he got off the train at the depot, as if he expected Mayor Whitlock with a welcoming committee and the town band to meet him. But for my money he was lucky the mayor wasn't there with an unwelcoming committee. And, if the town band had been there, they would have been playing a funeral march and not "Hail The Conquering Hero."

I know this sounds like a cruel thing to say about my own brother. But Tom was different from any other kid in town because he had a great brain and a money-loving heart. And, when you put them together, you get the youngest confidence man who ever lived. Tom was so smart that he'd skipped the fifth grade, so he was only twelve when he came home from the academy. But he had begun his career as a swindler at the age of eight. There wasn't a kid in town he hadn't swindled, including me. I guess that was why the only kids at the depot to meet him were me and our five-year-old foster brother, Frankie. Tom had also made fools out of a lot of adults in town with his great brain. I think that is why the only grownups to meet him were Papa, Mamma, my Uncle Mark, and Aunt Cathie. Aunt Bertha had remained at home to start preparing supper. She really wasn't our aunt. She had come to live with us after her husband died and was like one of the family.

After the hugs, kisses, and handshakes were over, Uncle Mark patted Tom on the shoulder. "It has been mighty dull around here while you've been gone," he said.

Uncle Mark should know. He was the town marshal and a deputy sheriff. He had spent a lot of time in the past telling people why he couldn't arrest Tom. The Great Brain always made sure he didn't break any laws when pulling off one of his swindles.

Papa stared steadily at Tom. "And you had better see to it that things stay that way, T.D.," he said.

Papa called all of us boys except Frankie by our initials. All male Fitzgeralds in our family had the same middle name of Dennis because it was a tradition. But for my money, Papa telling Tom to keep things dull was like telling a fellow standing in a rain storm not to get wet.

We left the depot and started walking up Main Street which, as in most Utah towns, was lined on both sides with trees planted by early Mormon pioneers. Adenville had a population of about two thousand Mormons, four hundred Protestants, and only about a hundred Catholics. We didn't have a Catholic church. Protestants and Catholics went to the Community Church. Papa often said that any church was better than no church at all. The only time we Catholics saw a priest was for one week out of the year when a Jesuit missionary priest came to town.

Adenville was one of the few towns our size that had electric lights and telephones. There were wooden sidewalks in front of the places of business. East of the railroad tracks were a couple of saloons, the Sheepmen's Hotel, the livery stable, a rooming house, and a couple of stores. But most of the places of business and the residential district were west of the railroad tracks.

We walked up a block, out of the business district, to our house. Uncle Mark and Aunt Cathie left us when we reached the gate of our white picket fence. Every time our house needed a new coat of paint, Papa would spend days deciding what color to use. I don't know why because Mamma always had the house painted white with green trim. We had a big front porch running the width of the house, and Aunt Bertha was waiting there to meet us. She was a big woman in her sixties with hands and feet as big as a man's. She kissed Tom and Sweyn on the cheeks.

"Supper will be ready by the time you boys wash up," she said.

Tom patted his stomach. "Can't be too soon for me," he said.

"Or me," Sweyn said.

All I can say is that the food at the academy must have been pretty bad. My brothers ate as if they were starving. They each had three helpings of fried chicken, mashed potatoes with cream gravy, and peas with carrots. And they each topped this off with three pieces of black-berry pie.

Everything was nice and dull, just the way Papa wanted it, as we all sat in the parlor after supper. Papa sat in his rocking chair smoking his after-dinner cigar. Mamma sat in her maple rocker with the light from the chandelier shining on her golden hair. I was the spitting image of Papa with dark curly hair and dark eyes. Sweyn was a blond like Mamma and named after our Danish maternal grandfather. He was fourteen at the time. Tom didn't look like Papa or Mamma unless you sort of put them to-gether. He was the only one in the family who had freck-les. He and Sweyn were sitting on the sofa with Aunt Bertha. Frankie and I were sitting on the oriental rug in front of the stone fireplace. Frankie had the biggest dark eyes and black hair that looked like wet coal. His parents and brother had been killed in a landslide in Red Rock Canyon. When Uncle Mark couldn't locate any relatives, Papa and Mamma adopted Frankie.

6

Tom and Sweyn talked about life at the academy for awhile. Then I guess Tom figured things had been nice and dull long enough and it was time to get Papa all riled up.

"When do you want me to start working with you at the *Advocate?*" he asked Papa.

Our father was editor and publisher of the *Adenville Weekly Advocate,* the only newspaper in town. He also did all the printing in Adenville.

"S. D. did a very good job last summer," Papa said. "I see no reason to change that."

"But you let him work with you after his first year at the academy," Tom protested. "What is fair for him is fair for me!"

"You can help out when we have a big printing job," Papa said. "Meanwhile you will have your share of the chores to do around the house."

Tom got a sour look on his face. "Sweyn didn't have to do any more chores after going to the academy," he said stubbornly.

"You will help J. D. with the chores during summer vacations," Papa said firmly, "until Frankie is old enough to do them. And that is final."

Tom knew there was no appealing one of Papa's decisions. And I knew his great brain was already at work on how to bamboozle me into doing his share of the chores, as he had several times in the past. But I was determined not to let it happen again.

The next morning after breakfast Tom and I walked from the back porch down the path leading to the combination coal-and-woodshed. We had a big backyard with a

8

vegetable garden on one side of the path and a playground on the other. The chicken coop was next to the coal-and-woodshed. Behind these buildings were our corral, our big barn, and our icehouse. There was an alley leading from the corral to the street.

Tom helped me fill up the woodboxes and coal buckets in the kitchen, parlor, and bathroom. Then we fed and watered our team of horses, our milk cow, Sweyn's mustang Dusty, and the chickens. When we finished, we sat on the top rail of the corral fence with Frankie.

Tom put his arm around my shoulders. "It is going to be tough on your pocketbook, J. D.," he said, "losing a dime a week during summer vacation."

Papa gave us each an allowance of ten cents a week for doing the chores. For doing all the chores while Tom was at the academy, he had been paying me twenty cents. Now I would have to split with Tom again. I know a dime doesn't sound like much but back in those days it would buy what it costs fifty cents to buy today.

"You're right," I said.

"Tell you what I'm going to do," he said. "I'm going to fix it so you get fifteen cents each week instead of just a dime."

I knew there had to be a catch in it. "Why?" I asked.

"Out of the goodness of my heart," he said. "I'm going to let you do all the chores and all it will cost you is five cents a week."

I knew from past experience that if I refused he would put his great brain to work on a plan to make me do all the chores anyway. I sure as heck wasn't going to be stupid enough to let that happen. Five cents a week was better than nothing.

"It's a deal," I said.

"Before we shake on it," Tom said, "Mamma and Papa are going to want to know why you are doing all the chores. This is what we will tell them. You volunteered to do all the chores because you need the extra money. Now shake on it."

We shook hands to seal the bargain.

Frankie stared at me with his big dark eyes. "How come you are paying Tom five cents a week for letting you do all the chores?" he asked.

"Because that is the deal we made," I said.

"It's not fair," Frankie said. "You should get the whole twenty cents for doing all the chores. I'll bet when I tell Mamma and Papa they will say I'm right."

Tom stared bug-eyed at Frankie. "What have we got here?" he demanded. "A little snitcher in the family? Don't you know, Frankie, that brothers never snitch on each other?"

"I'm not your real brother," Frankie said, smiling.

"All right," Tom said. "What do you want not to tell?"

"Instead of John giving you a nickel a week," Frankie said, "he should give it to me. I at least help him do the chores."

"How about splitting it?" Tom asked. "You get the nickel one week and I get it the next?"

"Nope," Frankie said, as he climbed down from the railing.

I think that was the first time in Tom's life that he hadn't been able to outsmart a kid. He looked as stunned as a boy who has just been told the school term has been increased from nine months to twelve months each year.

"Come back here," he yelled at Frankie, who was going toward the house. "You win. J. D. will give you the nickel each week."

Frankie stopped and turned around to look at me. "I'll help for my nickel," he said.

Tom watched Frankie run toward the house. "He is too little to help with the chores," he said.

"No, he isn't," I said. "Frankie was born and raised on a farm. He has been helping me with the chores ever since coming to live with us. He waters the livestock, and waters and feeds the chickens, and helps carry in kindling wood."

"In other words," Tom said, "he has been doing about one fourth of the chores."

"About," I said.

"And I suppose," Tom said, "that you've been paying him one fourth of the allowance each week for helping."

"Of course not," I said. "He volunteered to help for nothing."

Tom shook his head. "I am ashamed of you, J. D.," he said, "taking advantage of that poor little boy. By rights you owe Frankie a nickel a week for helping with the chores since Papa and Mamma adopted him. And that would amount to about a dollar and a half. Oh well, when I tell Papa about it I'm sure he'll make you give Frankie the dollar and a half."

"But he volunteered," I protested. "And besides you just told Frankie that brothers don't snitch on each other. I happen to be your flesh-and-blood brother."

"I don't consider this snitching at all," Tom said. "You took advantage of our little foster brother and should be punished for it."

11

I knew by the time The Great Brain got through telling about it that it would sound as if I had been beating Frankie with a horsewhip to make him help me with the chores.

"Please don't tell," I pleaded.

Tom thought about it for a moment. "I had to give up a nickel a week to Frankie not to tell," he said. "And I think you should be punished for taking advantage of a little boy. Suppose you give me a nickel a week not to tell and we'll consider that your punishment."

"It's a deal," I said gratefully. A nickel a week to Tom during the summer vacation would only come to about sixty-five cents. That was a lot better than having to give Frankie a dollar and a half, besides any punishment Papa would hand down.

I went with Tom and Frankie to Smith's vacant lot after lunch. Mr. Smith let us use the lot as a playground in exchange for keeping it clear of weeds. Most of the fellows were there getting ready for a game of baseball. They all acted as if they were glad to see Tom as they shook hands and said hello, although none of them had been at the depot to meet him. I guess they were both glad and sorry to know he was back in town. Tom had always been a leader and something exciting was always happening when he was around. And like Uncle Mark had said, things had been mighty dull with Tom away. I guess that's why they were glad to have him back. But there wasn't a kid there who hadn't been swindled at one time or another by The Great Brain and that's why they were sorry he was back in town. Tom had whipped every kid there

12

his age or older at one time or another. And for my money, there is nothing like trying to be friends with a boy you know can whip you.

Tom insisted they show him any new baseball equipment they had received while he was at the academy. Basil Kokovinis showed Tom his new Spalding League Model bat. Jimmie Peterson, who was my age, showed Tom the new baseball he'd gotten for his birthday. Danny Forester had a new infielder's glove he had received for Christmas. Danny was Tom's age and had something the matter with his left eye. The eyelid was always half closed unless Danny became excited. Then it would flip open. It was open as he proudly showed off his new glove. The rest of us had the same mitts and gloves as the year before.

Danny and Tom were team captains and chose up sides. Tom made me the catcher on his team because, if I do say so myself, I was a pretty darn good catcher. After both teams had been selected, Frankie pulled on Tom's pants leg.

"Why can't I play?" he asked.

"Because you're too little," Tom said. "You watch."

"When will I be old enough to play?" Frankie asked.

"Next year," Tom said. "I'll organize a couple of teams for kids your age."

Danny's team got to bat first. I knew right away that Tom hadn't been able to play any baseball at the academy. He was so wild that he was giving up bases on balls as if he had money bet on Danny's team. His curve ball wasn't breaking. We played our usual five innings and boy, oh, boy, did we get skunked, eighteen to four. Then it was time for the kids to go home to do the evening chores.

13

Tom held Frankie by the hand as we walked toward home. "That is a beaut of a baseball Jimmie has," he said.

"It should be," I said. "It's a genuine Spalding Double-seam baseball from Sears Roebuck."

"I've got a bat just like Basil's," Tom said. "But that is some infielder's glove Danny has. With its velvet-tanned buckskin and felt lining, it makes this old glove of mine look sick."

I knew from the conniving look on his face that he was going to put his great brain to work on how to get that baseball and glove.

"Those Jesuit priests at the academy sure as heck didn't make a Christian out of you," I said.

Tom stopped. "And just what do you mean by that?" he demanded.

"Just what I said," I came right back at him. "I know your great brain is working like sixty on how to swindle Jimmie out of his baseball and Danny out of his glove. And that, for my money, proves those priests didn't make a Christian out of you."

"Did you hear that, Frankie?" Tom asked.

"I heard," Frankie said.

Tom shook his head sadly. "Can you imagine my own brother saying I'm not a Christian?" he asked. "And if I don't put a stop to it, he will blab it all over town. Well, there is only one way to put a stop to that, Frankie. And that is to tell Papa and Mamma that J. D. is going around telling people that I'm not a Christian."

"I didn't mean it exactly that way," I protested.

"You wouldn't have said it if you didn't believe it," Tom said. "Good Lord, J. D., do you realize what it is

14

going to do to Papa and Mamma when you start telling people that I'm not a Christian? The adults in Adenville will put two and two together. They will start believing that Papa and Mamma must also be heathens and infidels. Our family will be disgraced. We will have to move to another town."

"I'm not going to tell anybody that you aren't a Christian," I pleaded.

"I'm going to make sure you don't," Tom said, "by telling Papa and Mamma all about it. Maybe if they take away your allowance for about six months and give you the silent treatment for a month, that will teach you not to run around town telling lies about me."

"Please don't tell," I begged. I knew by the time Tom got through he would make it sound as if I was going around town knocking on doors and shouting, "My brother is a heathen and infidel!" And I would be lucky if I only lost my allowance for six months and Papa and Mamma didn't speak to me for a month.

"You must be punished for saying such a terrible thing about your own brother," Tom said.

"Then you punish me," I cried.

"I might consider it," Tom said, "if I thought it would stop you from ever saying I wasn't a Christian again."

"It will," I promised. "Just name the punishment."

"The punishment must be severe enough to teach you a lesson," Tom said. "I've got it. Give me your basketball and backstop."

I was the most popular kid in town because I owned the only basketball and backstop. I had received them for Christmas, and Papa had nailed the backstop on the alley side of our woodshed. Kids came from all over town to take turns playing. I didn't really know why Tom wanted the basketball and backstop. I could only guess that he couldn't stand for any kid in town to own something he didn't, including his own brother.

"You can have them," I said gratefully. "And thanks for not telling."

Frankie had a puzzled look on his face. "Why are you thanking Tom for taking your basketball and backstop away from you?" he asked.

"It's worth it," I said. "It would break Papa's and Mamma's hearts if they knew I'd said my own brother wasn't a Christian."

Tom pointed at Frankie. "You had better give him something for not telling, too," he said.

"I'm surrounded by connivers," I cried, feeling like a tiny mouse cornered by two big tomcats. "All right, Frankie, name your price for not telling."

Frankie looked at Tom. "What do you think I should ask for?"

"At least a quarter," Tom said, grinning.

Frankie thought for a moment. "Nope," he said. "I want his jackknife."

They had me over a barrel. What could I do? I gave Frankie the jackknife.

"You are nothing but a couple of blackmailers," I complained bitterly.

Sometimes a fellow can get so plumb disgusted with himself that he wishes he'd never been born. The Great Brain had only been home about twenty-four hours and already he had cost me my basketball, my backstop, my jackknife, and ten cents a week allowance. They had muz-

16

zles for dogs to stop them from barking and biting people. Why in the heck didn't somebody invent a muzzle for fools like me, who didn't have sense enough to keep their big mouths shut?

That evening after supper Sweyn went to sit on the front porch of the Vinson home with his girl, Marie. Sweyn had disgraced Tom and me after his first year at the academy by going with a girl. In those days boys under sixteen played with boys and girls played with girls. And any boy under sixteen who went with a girl was considered a sissie. The fellows had really given Tom and me a bad time about it. At the rate Sweyn was going, he would be married before he was sixteen and having kids before he was old enough to shave.

Tom left to see Parley Benson about something soon after. I started playing checkers with Frankie but he didn't have his mind on the game. Finally he got up and walked over and put his hand on Papa's knee.

"What is a blackmailer, Papa?" he asked.

Papa looked surprised and put aside a magazine he was reading. "Where did you pick up a word like that?" he asked.

I thought for sure Frankie was going to spill the beans but he didn't.

"I heard a boy say it," he said. "What does it mean?"

"A blackmailer," Papa said, "is one of the most lowdown crooks there is. He finds out a secret about somebody and threatens to tell other people about it if the person doesn't pay him to be silent."

"Thanks, Papa," Frankie said.

17

We played checkers until bedtime. When we went up to our bedroom, Frankie took the jackknife from his pocket and handed it to me.

"I'm sorry I took it," he said. "I didn't know what a blackmailer was until Papa told me. But Tom must know and that makes him the most lowdown crook there is."

"Tom has been blackmailing me since I can remember," I said. "But it doesn't bother him a bit. He doesn't consider it blackmail. He says he is just using his great brain to outsmart people."

"Then maybe you're right," Frankie said, "and Tom isn't a Christian after all. When he came home for the Christmas vacation, I liked him a lot. I even liked him more than I did you. But now I don't think I like him anymore. But I love you, John."

I'm not a fellow for getting mushy but I couldn't help hugging him. But for all Tom's faults, he was my brother.

"You must not only like Tom," I said, "but also love him because no matter what he does, he is your foster brother."

"I'll try," Frankie said, "but I wish he was more like you."

And somehow that made the loss of my basketball and backstop and ten cents a week a little easier to bear.

CHAPTER TWO

The Tin Can Swindle

THE NEXT MORNING Tom went up to his loft in the barn. Papa and Mr. Jamison, the carpenter, had built the loft by nailing boards across the beam rafters at one end of the barn. They had also built a wall ladder to get up to the loft. It was originally intended for Sweyn, Tom, and me. But The Great Brain, in his usual style, had taken sole possession of it. He had removed the wooden wall ladder and made a rope ladder instead. That way he could climb up and pull the rope ladder after him, so nobody else could get up to the loft. He had an accumulation of stuff up there, ranging from a beer barrel he used as a table to the skull of an Indian that Uncle Mark had found in Skeleton Cave. Tom always went up to his loft when he wanted to put his great brain to work on some scheme.

I was pretty sure he was working on how to swindle Jimmie out of his baseball and Danny out of his glove. Tom came down from the loft just as Frankie and I were finishing the morning chores. He had a gunnysack with him as he came out of the barn.

"Follow him, Frankie, and see where he goes," I said.

Frankie followed Tom up the alley. I sat on the railing of our corral fence. Frankie returned in a little while and climbed up beside me.

"Tom is looking in people's trash barrels and taking out tin cans and putting them in the sack," Frankie told me.

I figured Tom's great brain had blown a fuse. I was convinced of it when he returned and started washing the labels off the cans in the corral water trough.

"What in the heck are you going to do with those tin cans?" I asked.

"Yeah, what?" Frankie said.

"I'm going to use them for an experiment in hypnotism," Tom said. "Are the kids coming over to play basketball today?"

"We played baseball yesterday," I said. "That means we'll play basketball today."

"You can use my basketball and backstop," Tom said.

"Aren't you going to play?" I asked.

"No, J. D.," he said. "I'll be busy learning how to hypnotize people."

Tom picked up his seven shining-clean cans and went into the barn. Frankie and I crept to the wall and peeked through a knothole. Tom had the seven cans lined up on a bale of hay. He was kneeling down beside it as if he were praying. Then he picked up a can and waved it back and forth in front of his face. I was now positive that Tom's great brain had cracked. I ran to the kitchen where Mamma and Aunt Bertha were kneading dough to make bread.

"Tom has gone crazy!" I shouted. "He's got seven tin cans lined up on the bale of hay in the barn and is waving them back and forth. He says it's an experiment in hypnotism."

"Nonsense," Mamma said. "Your brother is just pulling your leg."

Well, if Mamma didn't think a fellow who knelt down as if praying and waved tin cans in front of his face was insane, why should I?

Right after lunch Tom went into the barn again. Howard Kay, Jimmie Peterson, Seth Smith, Basil Kokovinis, Parley Benson, and Danny Forester arrived to play basketball.

Parley pushed the coonskin cap he always wore to the back of his head. "There are only seven of us," he said. "We need another player. Where is Tom?"

"In the barn trying to hypnotize some tin cans," I said.

"Nobody can hypnotize a tin can," Parley said.

"That is sure as heck what it looks like to me," I said.

"I've got to see this," Parley said.

I followed Parley and the other kids into the barn. Tom was again kneeling before the bale of hay with the seven shining tin cans on it.

"What are you doing?" Parley asked.

Tom looked up. "I'm learning how to hypnotize people," he said. "This is the first lesson in the book. Kneel down on the opposite side of the bale of hay and I'll show you how it is done."

Parley knelt down.

"We're going to take turns picking up the tin cans," Tom said. "I'm going to hypnotize you and make you pick up the last can."

"You don't have to hypnotize anybody to do that," Parley said. "There are seven tin cans. Whoever picks up the first one has to pick up the last one, if you take turns one at a time."

"That would be true," Tom said, "if you could only pick up one at a time. But you can pick up one or two cans at a time and so can I. And that means I would have to hypnotize you to make you pick up the last can."

"Sounds like a lot of bunk to me," Parley said. "And my Pa told me one time that you can't hypnotize anybody unless they let you."

"If you think I can't hypnotize you," Tom said, "put your money where your mouth is. I'll bet a nickel I can make you pick up the last can. And I'll bet every kid here I can hypnotize him and make him pick up the last can."

"It's a bet," Parley said.

Tom picked up a can and began waving it back and forth. "Keep your eyes on the can," he chanted. "Keep your eyes on the can. Now count backwards from ten to one."

"Ten," Parley said as his eyes followed the can, "nine, eight, seven, six, five, four, three, two, one."

23

"You are now hypnotized, Parley Benson," Tom chanted, "and under my power. You will do what I tell you to do until I snap my fingers and bring you out of it. You will pick up the last can. I'll go first."

"Oh, no you won't," Parley said, and he sure didn't look hypnotized to me. "I'll go first."

"Go ahead," Tom said. "But you are in my power and I command you to pick up two cans."

Parley was grinning as he picked up just one can. Tom then removed one can, leaving five.

"I command you to pick up two cans," Tom chanted.

Parley picked up just one, leaving four. Tom picked up one can leaving three.

"Pick up just one can," Tom ordered.

Parley picked up two cans, leaving Tom stuck with the last can. Tom had a long face as he gave Parley a nickel.

"It does say in the book that some people can't be hypnotized," he said. "Seth, you try it."

"I'm betting a nickel too," Seth said as he knelt down.

Tom went through the same ritual with Seth that he had with Parley. Seth went first and removed two cans from the bale of hay, leaving five. Tom took two, leaving three. Seth took two cans, leaving Tom stuck with the last can.

"It's just my luck," Tom said, "that I picked two people who can't be hypnotized." He gave Seth a nickel and then looked up at Basil. "You're next."

"I'm betting a nickel too," Basil said as he knelt down.

Tom went through the ritual. Basil took one can. Tom took one. Basil took one, leaving four. Tom took one.

"You are under my power, Basil Kokovinis," Tom chanted. "Take just one can."

Parley touched Basil on the shoulder. "Don't do it," he said. "If you take one, then he'll take one and you'll be stuck with the last can."

Basil removed two cans, leaving Tom stuck with the last can. Tom gave him a nickel.

I was beginning to feel sorry for Tom. I knew forking over those nickels was breaking his money-loving heart. And I was sure whoever sold him that book on hypnotism had swindled him.

"Maybe you, Parley, and Seth are all fellows who can't be hypnotized," Tom said. "Howard, you're next."

"Phooey on your hypnotism," Howard said, as he knelt down. "And I'm betting a dime you can't hypnotize me."

"But the other fellows only bet a nickel," Tom protested.

"You just said you'd bet us all," Howard said. "You didn't say how much. I'm betting a dime."

Again Tom went through the ritual. And again he ended up with the last can and had to pay Howard a dime. Then he stood up.

"No more bets," Tom said. "I've already lost twenty-five cents and that is enough. I have to study the book on hypnotism some more. I must be doing something wrong."

"You can't quit now," Danny said. "You promised to bet all of us and there is still me and Jimmie and John and Frankie."

"I don't believe my own brother and foster brother would want to take advantage of me," Tom said. "But I'll tell you what I'll do with you and Jimmie. If you let me go first, I'll bet. Maybe that is what I'm doing wrong."

"No you don't," Danny said. "You let the other kids go first and that means Jimmie and I go first."

"All right," Tom said, looking mighty angry. "But if you and Jimmie want to bet, you have to bet a dollar. Howard made me bet him a dime instead of a nickel. So I'm going to make you and Jimmie bet a dollar."

"You know darn well that Jimmie and I ain't got a dollar," Danny protested. "That's just your way of trying to weasel out of betting us."

"Then bet something that is worth a dollar," Tom said, "or forget the whole thing."

"This is one time we've all got you where we want you," Danny said, his left eyelid flipping open. "And it is going to cost you plenty to make up for all the times you swindled me. I'll bet anything I own that you can't hypnotize me and make me take the last can."

Tom thought about it for a moment. "Tell you what I'll do," he said. "That infielder's glove of yours cost about two dollars and a quarter from Sears Roebuck. How about betting your glove against what it cost?"

I guess that after seeing Tom couldn't hypnotize four other kids, Danny was pretty sure he couldn't be hypnotized.

"You said that thinking I wouldn't bet my glove," he said. "Well, you're wrong. It's a bet."

"That leaves Jimmie," Tom said. "I won't bet you unless Jimmie bets too. That baseball of his cost a dollar and ten cents. He is going to have to bet his baseball against my dollar and ten cents or I won't bet you, Danny."

"Boy, oh, boy," Danny said, "you are sure trying hard to get out of betting. But Jimmie will take the bet, won't you, Jimmie?"

26

Jimmie shook his head. "Gosh," he said, "I don't know if I should."

"Good," Tom said, smiling. "Then all bets are off."

Danny patted Jimmie on the shoulder. "Can't you see that Tom doesn't want to bet because he knows he is going to lose?" he asked. "The Great Brain knows darn well he can't hypnotize anybody. And the fellow who goes first has to win."

"All right," Jimmie said. "I'll bet."

Tom looked very disappointed. "Are you sure you want to bet, Jimmie?" he asked.

"I'm sure," Jimmie answered.

Tom looked like a fellow who just lost the ball game as he knelt down with Danny next to the bale of hay. He went through the same ritual, waving the can and making Danny count backwards from ten.

"You are now hypnotized, Danny Forester," Tom chanted. "You are under my power. I order you to make sure you take the last can."

Danny removed two cans. Tom took one, leaving four. Danny stared at the four cans and finally took one. Then Tom took two, leaving Danny stuck with the last can. Tom snapped his fingers.

"I did it!" he shouted. "I hypnotized you and made you take the last can."

Danny's left eyelid was wide open as he stared at Tom. "I don't feel hypnotized," he said.

"I brought you out of your hypnosis when I snapped my fingers," Tom said. "Come on, Jimmie, you're next."

"I changed my mind," Jimmie said.

"You can't change your mind," Tom said, "unless you want to be known as a welcher. And I don't know any kid in town who will have anything to do with a welcher."

I guess Jimmie didn't want to be known as a welcher. He knelt down by the bale of hay. Tom went through the ritual.

"You are now hypnotized, Jimmie Peterson," Tom chanted, "and under my power. I order you to make sure you take the last can."

Jimmie's hand was shaking as he removed one can. Tom took two, leaving four. Jimmie's hand was shaking even more as he took two cans. Tom then removed one can, leaving Jimmie stuck with the last can. Then he snapped his fingers.

"It just goes to prove," Tom said, "that some people can be hypnotized and some can't, just like it says in the book. Bring the baseball over any time tomorrow, Jimmie. And the same thing goes for the infielder's glove, Danny."

I sure couldn't help feeling sorry for Jimmie because he and Howard Kay were my two best friends. He looked as if he was going to cry.

"Let's play basketball," I said.

We played basketball until it was time for everybody to go home and do the evening chores. Tom carefully examined the basketball.

"This basketball cost two dollars and twenty cents," he said. "Playing on the ground instead of a hard wood floor is wearing it out."

Danny gave Tom a nasty look. "What skin is that off your nose?" he asked. "It is John's ball."

"No, it isn't," Tom said. "I made a deal with him for the basketball and backstop yesterday. You fellows sure as heck can't expect me to buy a new basketball every time one wears out. It is going to cost a penny a day for each kid who wants to play from now on. That way I'll have enough money to buy a new ball when this one wears out."

Basil shook his head. "I don't charge kids to use my new baseball bat," he said.

Jimmie nodded. "And I didn't charge to use my new baseball," he said.

"That's different," Tom said. "Whoever heard of a baseball bat wearing out? And you can use the baseball I won for nothing. But it is a penny a day to play basketball from now on."

The kids all grumbled about it. But I knew they would all pay because basketball was so much fun and such an exciting game. And I knew right then that The Great Brain was going to make me pay too.

That evening after supper Sweyn left to see his girl and Tom left the house also. Now that The Great Brain was twelve years old, he was allowed to remain outside the house until eight o'clock. I was in the parlor with Frankie and Papa while Mamma and Aunt Bertha were doing the supper dishes.

I only had a little brain but I didn't believe Tom could really hypnotize anybody. I figured if he could he'd be hypnotizing kids all over town and getting everything he wanted. I got the checkerboard and put seven checkers on it. I walked over to Papa.

"Tom showed me a trick today," I said, "but I can't figure out how he did it. The idea of the trick is to make the other player take the last checker. A player can take one checker or two checkers at a time."

I put the checkerboard on Papa's knees. He studied

the checkers for a moment, and Frankie came over to watch.

"It is a simple mathematical problem that T. D. probably learned in advanced arithmetic at the academy," Papa said. "Whoever goes first must lose."

"How do you figure that?" I asked.

"All the person going second has to do is to leave just four checkers," Papa explained. "You go first and I'll show you."

I removed one checker. Papa removed two.

"There are now four checkers left," Papa said. "No matter if you take one or two I can make you take the last checker. If you take one then I take two and you get the last checker. If you take two then I take one and you get the last checker."

"I understand that part," I said. "But Tom also made it so he always got the last checker."

"That is easy," Papa said as he lined up the seven checkers on the board. "You go first."

I removed one checker.

"Now all I have to do is to take the same number of checkers as you do," Papa said, "so I'll take one. There are five left. If you take one I take one leaving three. Then all you have to do is to take two and I get the last checker."

"What if I take two the first time?" I asked.

"That would leave five," Papa said. "Then I would take two leaving three. And all you have to do is to take two and I get the last checker."

"Thanks a lot, Papa," I said. "T. D. sure had me buffaloed on this trick."

I walked over and sat down on the floor with Frankie.

We played checkers until bedtime. Frankie didn't say what was on his mind until we reached our bedroom.

"Tom cheated Jimmie and Danny," he said.

"He doesn't call it cheating," I said. "According to Tom, he is simply using his great brain to get something he wants."

"I'm all mixed up," Frankie said. "I don't know who is right and who is wrong."

"You'll find out tomorrow," I said. "Danny's father will complain to Papa and Jimmie's mother to Mamma. It will then be up to The Great Brain to convince Papa and Mamma that he didn't cheat anybody."

When Papa came home for lunch the next day I knew Mr. Forester had complained from the way Papa kept looking at Tom during the meal. And I figured Mrs. Peterson must have complained too from the way Mamma kept staring at Tom. But Papa didn't say anything until we had finished eating.

"Well, T. D.," he said as he put his napkin in his silver napkin ring, "I see you are at it again. Mr. Forester stopped in at the *Advocate* office this morning. He told me that you had cheated his son Danny out of a baseball glove."

Mamma held up her hand. "Before you answer that, Tom Dennis," she said, "Mrs. Peterson phoned me this morning to complain that you had cheated her son Jimmie out of a new baseball."

Tom didn't appear worried at all. "Did Mr. Forester demand that you make me return the infielder's glove to Danny?" he asked Papa.

"Well, no, he didn't," Papa said.

31

Then Tom looked across the table at Mamma. "Did Mrs. Peterson insist that you make me give Jimmie back the baseball?" he asked.

"No, she didn't," Mamma answered. "But she was certainly upset about it."

"I think that proves I didn't cheat Danny or Jimmie," Tom said. "If I had cheated, they would have demanded that I return the glove and the baseball. And if Danny had won the two dollars and a quarter from me, you can bet his father wouldn't have mentioned it to you, Papa. And the same with Jimmie."

After that brilliant defense there was nothing Papa could do but nod his head. "You do have a point," he said.

"Point or no point," Mamma said, "Mrs. Peterson works very hard to support herself and her son. And a dollar-and-ten-cent baseball to her is the equivalent of a bicycle to your father and me."

"All the more reason why she should be thanking you instead of complaining," Tom said.

"And just how do you arrive at that conclusion?" Mamma asked.

"Assume Jimmie had won the dollar and ten cents from me," Tom said. "He would say to himself, look at all this money I won betting. This would make him want to bet some more, and he would get the gambling fever, which is worse than drink. Jimmie would grow up to be a gambling man, taking money from his poor mother to gamble away in the saloons. The same goes for Danny. So you see, if it weren't for me both Jimmie and Danny would have become gamblers, bringing sorrow, heartache, and disgrace to their families."

It is a rare occasion when a boy can dumbfound his parents so they just sit with open mouths and staring eyes. Aunt Bertha was the only one not struck dumb by Tom's brilliant logic.

"I do declare," she said, "if that boy was caught with his hand in the cookie jar, he would convince us he was putting a cookie back."

Tom excused himself from the table. Frankie and I joined him on the back-porch steps. Tom looked plumb disgusted.

"I just don't understand what made Papa and Mamma so upset," he said. "You would think they would be used to parents complaining about my great brain by this time."

"I know how you did it," I said. "I didn't snitch. I told Papa that it was a puzzle you showed me and used checkers instead of tin cans. Papa said it was a mathematical problem you must have learned in class at the academy."

"He was wrong about that," Tom said. "I learned the trick from a kid named Jerry Moran at the academy."

"Why did you go through all that rigmarole with the tin cans and pretending you could hypnotize people?" I asked.

"Jerry showed me the trick with seven pennies," Tom said. "But if I'd used pennies and offered to bet I could make the kids take the last one, they would have known it was a trick right away. Those kids weren't betting I couldn't make them take the last can. They were betting I couldn't hypnotize them."

"It was still a swindle," I said.

"Wrong," Tom said. "When Parley, Seth, Basil, and

Howard bet me, they were all positive they had a sure thing. And they won twenty-five cents from me. Do you think they swindled me out of my quarter?"

"Well, no," I had to admit.

"And when Danny and Jimmie bet," Tom said, "they were positive they had a sure thing and couldn't lose. If they had won the three dollars and thirty-five cents from me, would you say they had swindled me?"

"Of course not," I answered.

"Then how can you say I swindled them because I was positive that I had a sure thing?" Tom demanded.

I thought about it for a moment. "I guess you didn't swindle them after all," I had to admit.

"I accept your apology," Tom said.

Frankie smiled at Tom. "Then you didn't cheat," he said as if the idea pleased him.

Tom ruffled Frankie's hair with his fingers. "You can't be guilty of cheating somebody," he said, "if that person is trying to cheat you."

Well, all I can say is that The Great Brain could talk himself out of anything. If he was caught stealing a horse, he would claim he was nearsighted and thought it was his lost milk cow. And for my money, he would get away with it.

CHAPTER THREE

The Tug of War

TOM DIDN'T MAKE AS MUCH money as I thought he would charging the kids to play basketball because soon we were able to go swimming. The first thing every kid looked forward to when summer vacation began was the day he could go swimming in the river. We seldom got any cold weather in Adenville during the winter because the town was located in southwestern Utah. But it did snow in the mountains west of Adenville. Until after that snow melted, the water in the river was too cold for swimming. So it was a great day for all the boys in town when we saw all the snow in the mountains was gone.

Tom and I were late getting to the swimming hole

that afternoon because of Frankie. He wanted to go swimming with us and take along his playmate, Eddie Huddle.

"You are too little to go swimming," Tom said.

Frankie began to cry. "You always say I'm too little," he cried. "Too little to play baseball. Too little to play basketball. Now I'm too little to go swimming."

"Stop bawling," Tom said. "If Mamma says you can go, we will take you with us."

Mamma surprised us by saying Frankie could go if we would watch out for him. She hadn't let me go until I was seven years old. Then Eddie Huddle began to bawl.

"I wanna go swimmin' too," he cried. "If Frankie goes I ain't got nobody to play with."

Frankie put his arm around Eddie's shoulders. "If Eddie can't go," he said to Tom and me, "I won't go. And if I don't go after Mamma telling you to take me, it means you can't go."

What could Tom and I do? We walked to the blacksmith shop owned by Eddie's father. Mr. Huddle said we could take Eddie if we kept a careful eye on him.

There were about fifty kids at the swimming hole. We all went swimming naked because nobody owned a bathing suit then. I had learned how to swim when Sweyn tossed me into the deepest part of the swimming hole from the diving board. But Frankie and Eddie were too young for this. Tom and I showed them how to pretend they were swimming by mud crawling. They could walk on their hands in the shallow water and, by kicking their legs, keep their bodies afloat. Tom and I took turns watching them. I knew from the fun the two kids were having that we would be stuck taking them swimming all summer.

After swimming in the river began, the next thing we all looked forward to was the Fourth of July. Nobody in Adenville ever locked their barns until one week before the Fourth. Then suddenly the barns of everybody who was going to enter a float in the Fourth-of-July parade became forbidden territory. This was because people were secretly working on their floats. No one got to see the floats until the morning of the parade.

The first prize was a blue ribbon with the words "First Prize" printed on it. The second prize was a red ribbon and third prize a white ribbon. I doubt if these ribbons cost more than twenty-five cents each. But the way people worked on floats, you would have thought the ribbons were worth a fortune. Mamma had won one blue ribbon, two red ribbons, and two white ribbons over the years. This Fourth of July she was determined that she was going to win first prize.

And this Fourth of July Tom had made up his mind that the Gentile kids were going to win the tug of war. I'd better explain that back in those days anybody who wasn't a Mormon was called a Gentile in Utah. Every Fourth, ten Mormon kids and ten Gentile kids between the ages of eleven and twelve were chosen for the tug of war. The kids themselves selected the biggest and strongest boys for their teams. A rope was stretched across Aden Irrigation Canal, which was about three feet deep and ten feet wide and ran down one side of the town park. The teams lined up on each side of the canal. Then the tug of war began to see which team could pull the other into the canal.

The Gentile kids had been getting dunked in the canal ever since I could remember. It didn't take a great brain to figure out why. The Mormon kids outnumbered the Gentile kids in town by about four to one. This gave them a four-to-one advantage in picking the biggest and strongest kids for their team. That is why I thought Tom had suddenly came down with brain fever when he said he was going to put his great brain to work on how to win the tug of war. I knew even his great brain couldn't make ten Gentile kids each grow ten pounds heavier and stronger in a week.

Mamma had a beaut of an idea for a float. She told us about it one night after supper.

"My entry is going to be entitled *The Ringing of the Liberty Bell*," she said, looking mighty pleased.

Papa nodded. "An excellent idea," he said. "But you would need some sort of a belfry to hang the bell on. And I doubt if there is room enough in our buggy."

"Mark is going to let us borrow his wagon," Mamma said. "We'll move the buggy out of the barn and the wagon into it tomorrow."

"That problem is solved," Papa said, "but what are you going to use for a bell? We can't use the town hall bell because it is used to summon the volunteer fire department in case of fire. And I doubt if Reverend Holcomb would want us to take the bell from the Community Church."

"You are forgetting the schoolhouse bell," Mamma said.

"Right," Papa said. "I'm sure I can get Calvin Whitlock and the other two members of the school board to let us borrow the bell."

"No," Mamma said, to our surprise. "Mrs. Granger is a member of the school board and enters a float every year. I don't want her to know about my idea. She might want to copy it and take the bell for her own float. You will just have to get the bell without permission from anybody. And wait until the evening of July third to do it."

"Another excellent idea," Papa said.

Well, all I can say is that it just goes to prove there is no figuring grownups. If Sweyn and Tom and I had told Papa and Mamma that we were going to steal the schoolhouse bell, they would have had a fit about it. Just for saying it we would have lost our allowances for six months. But there sat Papa and Mamma smiling proudly, as if stealing a schoolhouse bell wasn't any crime at all. Their consciences weren't bothering them a bit. Try and figure that one out because I can't.

Uncle Mark's wagon was moved into our barn the next day. Papa bought some lumber. Tom, Sweyn, and I helped him build a belfry on the bed of the wagon. The next day Mamma and Aunt Bertha began decorating the wagon. They wove red, white, and blue bunting between the spokes of the wheels and draped it around the body of the wagon and the seat. After the wagon was decorated, Mamma and Aunt Bertha began making the costumes my brothers and I would wear.

On the evening of July third Papa was nervous. Instead of smoking just one after-dinner cigar, he smoked two. Mamma kept looking out the bay window in the parlor. Finally she spoke.

"It is dark now; time to go get the bell," she said as if Papa went out stealing schoolhouse bells every night of the week.

Papa cleared his throat. "I've decided to take Sweyn and Tom with me," he said. "I might need some help."

"Can I go, too?" I asked.

Papa must have wanted all the company he could get when he went out stealing bells. He said I could go with them. We left by the back door and went to the toolshed for a wrench. Papa motioned for us to follow him into the barn. He sat down on a bale of hay and began patting my dog Brownie and Frankie's pup Prince on their heads.

"How much do you think that bell weighs?" he asked.

"About twenty pounds," Tom said.

"I've been thinking," Papa said. "If I'm caught removing the bell from the schoolhouse, it will make me the laughingstock of everybody in town. I'll be the butt of jokes for years to come. Now you boys don't want to see that happen to your father, do you?"

What could we say after that dramatic appeal? We all said we wouldn't want that to happen. And I knew right then why Papa wanted company when it came to stealing the bell.

"Thank you, boys," Papa said. "I'll just sit here and keep the dogs company while you go get the bell."

"If we get the bell for you, what do we get?" Tom asked.

"My undying thanks," Papa said.

"And if we let Mamma think you helped to get the bell?" Tom asked.

"I see what you mean," Papa said. "In addition to my undying thanks, you will each receive fifty cents."

"You've got yourself a deal, Papa," Tom said.

Tom got Sweyn's lariat and a gunnysack. He put the lariat and wrench in the sack. He acted as scout, leading

Sweyn and me down alleys and through vacant lots to the schoolhouse. Tom tried the door. It was locked.

"Now why would anybody be stupid enough to lock the door of a schoolhouse in the summertime?" he asked. "No kid in his right mind would enter a schoolhouse unless he had to."

"One of the windows isn't locked," I said, "unless they fixed it. Mr. Standish complained because he couldn't shut it last winter when it got a little cold."

I showed Tom and Sweyn the window, which was open about two inches. Tom pushed it up.

"You stay here, J. D.," he said, "and keep a sharp lookout."

I watched my two brothers climb through the window with the gunnysack. I kept a sharp lookout but didn't know what for. All I saw was a stray dog.

I knew exactly what my two brothers would have to do to get the bell. In the hallway where the kids hung their coats and caps during school, there was a ladder nailed to the wall that led to the belfry trap door. Once they got into the belfry, Tom would have to tie the clapper of the bell with a piece of twine he'd brought along so the bell wouldn't ring. Then they would have to loosen the U bolt holding the bell. Once they got the bell on the floor of the belfry, they could tie one end of the lariat to it and lower it down into the hallway.

It seemed to me they were taking a long time but they finally came to the window. They had the bell, wrench, and lariat in the gunnysack. Tom climbed out the window and Sweyn handed him the gunnysack.

"You scout, J. D.," Tom said. "S. D. and I will carry the gunnysack."

I scouted and got us back to the barn without anybody seeing us. Papa had lit the kerosene lantern we kept in the barn and was sitting on a bale of hay, patting the heads of Brownie and Prince. He got up and helped my two brothers hang the bell on the homemade belfry on the wagon while I held the lantern. Then Papa stood back and admired the float.

"Don't forget, boys," he said. "Mum's the word to your mother." Papa wanted to make sure he got credit for stealing the bell.

"Aren't you forgetting something?" Tom asked, grinning.

Papa took out his purse and gave each of us half a dollar. It made me wonder how many things Papa had done that Mamma didn't know anything about.

Tom touched my arm. "Leave the dogs in the barn," he whispered.

I didn't know why he wanted me to leave the dogs in the barn, but I did. It was past my bedtime when we entered the house.

"The bell is on the float," Papa told Mamma and Aunt Bertha, looking as proud as if he had done it all by himself.

I'm telling you, Papa was really something sometimes. But I didn't mind him taking all the credit. I was fifty cents richer than when I left the house. I went upstairs with Tom.

"Keep your clothes on," Tom said. "We're going out. That's why I told you to leave the dogs in the barn. We don't want them following us. And be quiet so you don't wake up Frankie."

"Where are we going?" I whispered.

"To fix it so those Mormon kids lose the tug of war tomorrow," he said.

"Do you mean your great brain figured out a plan to dunk those Mormon kids in the canal?" I asked.

"I'll not only dunk them," Tom said, "but empty their pocketbooks at the same time."

He removed the screen from our bedroom window, and we shinnied down the elm tree by the window. I followed him to the woodshed. He picked up a partly filled gunnysack and the ax and a shovel.

"What's in the sack?" I asked.

"Wooden stakes," he answered. "And stop asking questions. We have work to do."

Just then the whistle at the powerhouse blew, signaling that it was nine o'clock and curfew time. No kid under sixteen was allowed on the streets after nine o'clock unless accompanied by an adult. This meant Tom and I had to be careful. I followed him down alleys on a roundabout way to the town park. The park was one block square with a bandstand in the middle and picnic tables set under trees. It was bounded on one side by the Aden Irrigation Canal. Tom and I cut through the park to the bridge over the canal. We crossed the bridge and walked about fifteen feet below it to where the tug of war was always held. Tom dumped out the stakes from the gunnysack. They had sharp points on one end and were about two inches thick and eight inches long.

Tom picked up one of the stakes and drew two lines in the dirt about a foot apart, straight out from the canal for about twenty-five feet.

"This is the path my team will use for the tug of war," he said. "Take the shovel and scoop out the dirt down about three inches. I'm going to drive stakes in the ground about six inches apart, all along the path my team will use. We will be able to brace our heels against the stakes and it would take a team of mules to pull us across the canal. We will just hold the Mormon team until they get good and tired. Then, using the stakes as anchors to brace the heels of our shoes against, we will pull them across the canal."

"Won't they see the stakes?" I asked.

"No," he said, "because I'll cover them up with about an inch of dirt."

"Then why do you want me to dig down three inches?" I asked.

"So the dirt will be loose to dig the heels of our shoes into," Tom said. "The stakes will still have to be driven about six inches into solid ground so they will hold."

I began scooping out the dirt with the shovel between the lines Tom had drawn. He came right behind me, hammering the stakes into the ground with the blunt end of the ax. When we had finished we covered up the stakes with dirt so they couldn't be seen.

I was much too excited about the float contest the next morning to think about the tug of war. We braided red, white, and blue ribbons into the manes of our horses, after hitching them to the wagon. We fastened tassles to the harnesses and small American flags to the hames of the harnesses. Mamma used a black crayon to put an imitation crack on the bell. Then we went into the house to put on our costumes. Sweyn would drive the team dressed in a red, white, and blue Uncle Sam costume Mamma and Aunt Bertha had made. My costume was the kind of clothing a boy wore in 1776 and Tom's the kind of clothing an old man wore then. To make Tom look like an old man, Mamma had made a white wig and beard out of cotton. At last we were ready to take the float to the campground.

I could hear kids shooting off firecrackers all over town as we left our barn. Sweyn was driving the team and Tom and I were in our places on the float. Uncle Mark was in charge of lining up the floats at the campground. He was riding his stallion, Lightning, and wearing a white Stetson hat, a bright red shirt, white buckskin pants, and a red, white, and blue scarf around his neck. He directed Sweyn to our place in the line of floats.

There were about twenty floats entered. Right in front of us was Seth Smith's mother's float, depicting Washington crossing the Delaware. She must have been sewing for weeks. Mr. Smith was wearing a uniform and hat like photographs I'd seen of General George Washington. His brother and a couple of other relatives were dressed like soldiers in the Continental Army. Mr. Smith and his brother had built a pretty good imitation of a boat on the bed of their wagon. Behind us was Mrs. Winters' float, showing Betsy Ross making the first American flag.

Uncle Mark, acting as grand marshal, signaled that the parade was about to begin. He rode at the head of it, carrying a large American flag. Behind him on foot was the town band playing "Columbia the Gem of the Ocean." They were wearing white flannel trousers, white shirts, and straw hats with red, white, and blue ribbons on them. Main Street was a glorious sight with all the buildings decorated with red, white, and blue bunting and American flags. Men, women, and children lined both sides of the street waving small flags and brightly colored balloons.

The judges' stand was a platform that had been built in front of the Adenville bank. The three judges were Mayor Whitlock, Judge Potter, and Bishop Aden of The Church of Jesus Christ of Latter-day Saints, which was the full name of the Mormon church. Bishop Aden was the founder of Adenville, for whom the town was named.

Uncle Mark stopped the parade as each float reached the judges' stand. When it was Mrs. Smith's turn, I just knew she was going to win first prize. The applause from the judges and spectators for Washington crossing the Delaware was so loud, I could hardly hear the band.

"Ready, J. D.?" Tom asked.

I nodded my head. A moment later Sweyn stopped our team in front of the judges' stand.

"Ring, Grandpa, ring!" I shouted, just the way Mamma had coached me. "Oh, ring for liberty!"

Tom began pulling the rope that rang the schoolhouse bell. And it sounded to me as if our float got as much applause as Mrs. Smith's float.

The parade continued down Main Street, passing our home, and on to West Tenth Street, where it broke up. The prizes wouldn't be awarded until that afternoon. It was time to take the float home. Papa was waiting in the corral for us. He, Mamma, and Aunt Bertha had watched the parade from our front porch.

We unhitched the team from the wagon and hitched it to our buggy. Then Tom, Sweyn, and I went into the house to take off our costumes and put on our everyday clothes. Everybody got all dressed up for the parade, but after it was over all the boys and girls changed to their everyday clothing so they could enter the contests.

46

We all began loading up the buggy for the picnic. First came the washtub with a cake of ice in it and a watermelon and bottles of homemade root beer. Then came baskets, pots, and pans containing food. The ice-cream freezer was last, after being repacked with salt and ice.

There wasn't room in the buggy for all of us to ride. Papa took Mamma and Aunt Bertha with him. Tom, Sweyn, Frankie, and I walked to the park after getting our firecrackers and sparklers from the house. There were buggies and wagons with teams of horses parked on both sides of the streets. Papa found a place to leave our buggy while Mamma found a picnic table under a tree for us. We all helped unload the food. Like all Adenville families we would spend the rest of the day in the park.

Every picnic table was piled high with about the same things we had on our table. There were bowls filled with fried chicken and potato salad. There were plates with green onions, radishes, pickles, olives, and hard-boiled eggs. There was a big smoked ham and bread-and-butter sandwiches. And, for dessert, we had an apple and berry pie, chocolate cake, ice cream, and watermelon.

I ate until I thought I would burst and so did everybody else in the park. Then the picnic tables were covered with tablecloths to protect the food from flies, and we all crowded around the bandstand. The band played a fanfare. Then Mayor Whitlock held up his hands for silence.

"Ladies and gentlemen," he said, "the moment you have all been anxiously waiting for has arrived. But first, the judges wish to compliment the persons responsible for so many fine floats this year. They made the decision

of the judges very difficult. After due deliberation, however, the judges have awarded first prize to Mrs. Smith for
her float showing Washington crossing the Delaware."

The crowd applauded as Mrs. Smith went up to the
bandstand to get her blue ribbon. Again Mayor Whitlock
held up his hands for silence.

"The judges have awarded Mrs. Fitzgerald second
prize for her float depicting the ringing of the liberty bell,"
he announced.

I could see Mamma was happy as she went to get her
red ribbon. Not as happy as she would have been to win
first prize, but happy. But it just goes to prove that the
more a kid tries to figure out how the minds of grownups
work, the more confused he becomes. Mayor Whitlock
must have known that the bell on Mamma's float was the
schoolhouse bell. And as chairman of the school board he
certainly knew the bell had been taken without his permission. But instead of having Mamma arrested for stealing the bell, there was Mayor Whitlock awarding her
second prize. Boy, oh, boy, you can bet if some kids had
stolen the bell the Mayor would have had them arrested.

Mrs. Carter was awarded third prize for her float de-
picting the signing of the Declaration of Independence.
It was then time for the contests for kids to begin, with
Reverend Holcomb and Bishop Aden acting as judges and
Uncle Mark as starter. Grownups who didn't want to
watch the contests could listen to the band concert.

First came the spoon-and-egg races for kids five to six
years old. Each kid was given a spoon with a raw egg in it.
He or she had to hold the spoon by the handle. The first
one to reach the finish line without dropping the egg won.

"Don't run," I whispered to Frankie. "The kids who

try to run will drop their eggs. You just walk."

It was good advice but a couple of other kids had the same idea and one of them won the race. The egg-and-spoon races then continued for different age groups. Howard Kay won the race for my age group.

Then came the potato-sack races. Each kid put his feet and legs in a potato sack and, holding the sack around his waist, jumped toward the finish line. Frankie lost because he fell down. I might as well have fallen down. I came in sixth for my age group. I began to wonder why Tom wasn't there. He had won the potato-sack race for three straight years. And this year the prize was a harmonica. All prizes for the races were donated by the merchants in town, but they were usually only worth about a nickel or dime at the most. The harmonica was worth at least a quarter. I became so curious that I went looking for Tom. Maybe he didn't know the prize was a harmonica.

I found him talking to some Mormon kids. He was making bets with them on the tug of war and writing down the amount and the names in a notebook. I told him about the harmonica prize.

"I'm not entering any contests this year," he said. "I've got a lot of kids to see before the tug of war."

I returned to the contests. I surprised myself by winning the foot race for kids my age. The prize was a box of Cracker Jacks which I gave to Frankie. When the contests were over, it was time to eat again. Everybody returned to their picnic tables. After eating Tom took me to one side.

"Hold on to this," he said, handing me the notebook. "It has all the bets I made in it. I don't want to get it wet in case we lose."

49

"How can you lose with those stakes in the ground?" I asked.

"I forgot something," Tom said. "Mayor Whitlock always tosses a coin to see which team gets which side of the canal. I've got to put my great brain to work on how to make sure my team gets the right side."

It was now time for the kids to shoot off their fire-crackers and sparklers and play games while the grownups listened to the band concert. This went on until it was time for the tug of war which was the last event of the day. A fanfare from the band notified everybody that the time had arrived. Mayor Whitlock was on the bandstand.

"Will the captains for the two teams come up here," he said.

Tom and Seth Smith went to the bandstand. The mayor removed a coin from his pocket.

"Excuse me, Mr. Whitlock," Tom said. "As you know, it is easier to get a good footing in the dirt on the other side of the canal than it is on the grass on this side. Don't you think it would be more fair to let the team that lost last year have the other side, instead of tossing a coin?"

Mr. Whitlock nodded. "I think that is a good idea," he said. "Is that all right with you, Seth?"

"It doesn't make any difference to my team," Seth said confidently. "We will win no matter which side we get."

Tom's great brain had done it again. He got the side where the stakes were for his team. He and Seth were given the rope for the tug of war. Tom held one end of it and crossed the bridge over the canal. He and Seth held the rope tight so it wouldn't get wet in the canal as they walked down to where the tug of war would take place.

50

Seth made Tubby Ralston his anchor man, tying his end of the rope around the fat boy's waist. Tom made Basil his anchor man. The other nine members of each team got in place and took a tight grip on the rope.

"All right, boys!" Uncle Mark shouted as he removed his Colt .45 from its holster and pointed it upwards. "Get ready! Get set! Go!" And he fired a shot into the air.

I watched the fellows on Tom's team dig their heels into the dirt. The Mormon team pulled them toward the canal a few inches, until the heels of the Gentile boys hit the stakes in the ground. Then Tom's team just stiffened their bodies and leaned back. Those Mormon kids puffed and heaved and grunted and groaned but they couldn't budge the Gentile team one inch. Tom just let them struggle until sweat was pouring off them and they were so tired their tongues were hanging out.

Then Tom shouted, "Now, men!"

The Gentile team began backing up, using the stakes in the ground to brace their feet. Slowly but surely they pulled the Mormon team toward the canal. Seth, as captain of the team, was the first to be pulled into the canal. And then the rest of those Mormon kids were dunked.

The Mormon team was the most downhearted bunch of kids I'd ever seen as they climbed out of the canal. The Gentile team was proud and happy as they danced around on the other side. But I knew the dancing was a part of Tom's plan. His team were using their feet to cover up the stakes with dirt.

Everybody went home after the tug of war. There were still two big events to come after supper. The fireworks display would begin on the courthouse lawn when it got dark, to be followed by a dance in the social hall of

the Mormon tabernacle. I guess every Mormon kid in town had bet on the tug of war. Tom totaled up the bets in the notebook when we got home. He had taken those Mormon kids for five dollars and fifteen cents. I was kicking myself that I was such a dumb-dumb, I didn't have sense enough to make a few bets myself.

After it got dark we all went to watch the fireworks. Uncle Mark was in charge of the display, which always lasted about an hour. It had always been the best part of the Fourth of July for me. Imagine my surprise when Tom pulled me aside just before the fireworks.

"I'll need your help for about half an hour," he said.

"If you think I'm going to miss the fireworks," I said, "you're crazy."

"You'll only miss half of it," he said, "and besides, I'll pay you a quarter. We've got to get those stakes out of the ground and this is the time to do it. Everybody in town is here. Now just sort of walk with me as if we were looking for a better spot to watch at the rear of the crowd."

I wasn't about to pass up a chance to make twenty-five cents, so I went with Tom. We got away from the crowd without being noticed. Then we ran home and got a gunnysack, a shovel, and the ax. When we arrived on the bank of the canal, I scooped the dirt away from the stakes with the shovel. Tom used the blunt end of the ax to knock the stakes loose and then put them in the gunnysack. After removing all the stakes, we smoothed out the dirt.

"Now jump around on the ground," Tom said.

"Why?" I asked.

"We've got to leave footprints just in case somebody does come snooping around," he said.

I understood as I remembered how the Gentile team were dancing around after winning. We made footprints and then went home. Tom mixed the stakes in with the chopped kindling wood in the woodshed. We got back to the courthouse before the loudest, most brilliant, and best of the fireworks were shot into the air. After the display was over, Papa and Mamma and Sweyn and his girl went to the dance in the Mormon tabernacle. Aunt Bertha, Frankie, Tom, and I went home.

Seth Smith and the nine other Mormon kids on the tug of war team came down the alley the next morning, just as Frankie and I were finishing our chores. Tom was sitting on the railing of the corral fence. He jumped to the ground and stared at the shovel Seth was carrying. Then he pulled the notebook from his pocket.

"I was just going to start making the rounds to collect the bets I won," he said.

"You aren't going to collect any bets," Seth said, "until we find out something."

"Like what?" Tom asked, looking innocent.

"Like how you beat us in the tug of war," Seth said. "I think you planted rocks and bricks in the ground on your side for your team to brace their feet against."

"I give you my word of honor," Tom said, "that we didn't put any rocks or bricks in the ground to brace our feet against. But if it will make you feel better, we will go take a look."

Eddie Huddle arrived to play with Frankie. I went with Tom and the Mormon kids to the canal. Seth dug up the ground every place a Gentile kid could have put his feet during the tug of war.

"Are you satisfied?" Tom asked.

Seth nodded his head.

"Then apologize for what you said," Tom ordered, "or you and I are going to have a fight right now."

Seth knew darn well he couldn't whip Tom. "Well, gee whiz," he said, "you can't blame me for being suspicious. You and I are about the only two the same size. All the other kids on my team were bigger and stronger than the kids on your team. We should have won easy."

"Do you call that an apology?" Tom demanded.

"All right," Seth said. "I'm sorry for what I said."

"That's better," Tom said. "And now that you've apologized, I'll tell you why your team lost. Every year the Mormon team has been winning the tug of war. This built up a lot of false confidence in your team. They were so sure they would win, some of them didn't even try. It stands to reason that with a heavier and stronger team you should have won, if every kid did his best. But some of them just lay down on the job, letting the others do the work." Tom took his notebook from his pocket. "I'll start collecting bets now and begin with you, Seth."

But The Great Brain didn't get to collect any bets right away. That little speech of his started the ten Mormon kids arguing with each other. They were accusing each other of lying down on the job. Words soon led to blows and in a few minutes there were five separate fist fights going on at the same time.

Tom stood watching with an amused smile on his face. "Enjoy it, J. D.," he said. "This makes up for all the times Mormon kids have dunked Gentile kids in the canal."

56

CHAPTER FOUR

Tom Hooks a Fish Named Sweyn

SWEYN HAD RECEIVED a fly rod and reel with a dozen fly hooks for Christmas. And now that it was fishing season, boy, oh, boy, did he think he was something. He took an old hat and put his fly hooks on it to make him look like a real fisherman. He placed a wooden hoop from a barrel on our front lawn and practiced casting inside the hoop. He went fishing in the river and caught plenty of suckers, but he had to throw them back. Mamma wouldn't cook them because she said they weren't fit to eat. Once in a while Sweyn did catch a rainbow or German brown trout in the river. But the only really good fishing around Adenville was in the creeks and streams in the mountains.

I couldn't blame Sweyn for being proud of his fishing gear. He was the only boy in town who had a fly rod and reel. The rest of us kids had to use just a pole with a line and hook. But I did blame Sweyn for being too darn selfish with his fishing gear. He wouldn't let Tom or me touch it, let alone practice casting.

Papa told us we would be leaving on our annual fishing and camping trip the week after the Fourth of July. Right away Sweyn began bragging that he would catch twice as many fish as Tom and me put together.

"You know, J. D.," Tom said to me the day before we were to leave, as we sat on the back porch steps, "when a fellow gets so selfish he won't let his own brothers touch his rod and reel, it is time to teach him a lesson."

I knew right then that Tom was going to put his great brain to work on a plan to stop Sweyn from being so selfish and a braggart.

That evening Tom was studying the pages advertising fishing gear in the Sears Roebuck catalog. Finally, he put it aside.

"Why do people pay so much money for fishing rods and reels?" he asked Papa.

Papa laid aside the magazine he had been reading. "The answer is obvious," he said. "To enable them to catch more fish. With a fly rod and reel, you can cast a line several times farther than you can with just a pole. This enables you to fish in waters you can't reach with a pole. With a fly rod you can also fish in rapids, where it is rather difficult to fish with a pole. And your chances of losing a fish you've hooked are slight. With a rod and reel you can let out line and play the fish and keep him hooked."

"In other words," Tom said, "S. D. should catch a lot more fish than I do on our trip."

"Considerably more," Papa answered.

"Will he catch a bigger fish?" Tom asked.

"It stands to reason that if he catches five or six times more fish than you do," Papa said, "he will catch a bigger fish than you do."

Tom shook his head. "I wouldn't be surprised if I catch a bigger trout than he does," he said.

Sweyn grinned. "Wouldn't want to bet on it, would you?" he asked.

"I just might," Tom said.

Then Papa said, "You would be very foolish if you did."

Frankie and I had to go to bed at eight o'clock. I was asleep when Tom and Sweyn came into the room at nine. Tom woke me up.

"Need you as a witness, J. D.," Tom said. Then he turned to Sweyn. "Now, big brother, put your money where your mouth is. Papa said the odds were five or six to one that you will catch a bigger fish on this trip than I will. Just give me odds of two to one and I'll make you a bet."

"You've got it," Sweyn said. "How much do you want to bet?"

"That Bristol steel fly rod of yours cost three dollars and ninety cents in the Sears Roebuck catalog," Tom said. "The Penell reel costs two dollars and fifty cents and a dozen hooks cost a dollar. That comes to seven dollars and forty cents. I'll bet three dollars and seventy cents against them that I catch a bigger trout on this trip than you do."

"That would make up for some of the cash you've won

from me in the past," Sweyn said. "But how do I know you won't borrow Dad's rod and reel?"

"J. D. is a witness," Tom said, "that I will use just a pole, line, and hook and worms for bait."

"Are we betting how long the fish is or by the weight?" Sweyn asked.

"By the weight," Tom answered. "We will take that old kitchen scale of Mamma's that she used to use for measuring flour with us."

"You've got yourself a bet," Sweyn said confidently.

"Shake on it," Tom said. "J. D. is a witness."

They shook hands to seal the bargain and then Sweyn went to his room.

"Boy, oh, boy," I said, "this is one time your great brain is going to cost you plenty. Papa said you'd be a fool to bet you would catch a bigger fish."

Tom grinned. "There is more than one way to hook a big fish," he said mysteriously.

We left the next morning. Tom and I rode in the buggy with Papa. Sweyn rode his mustang, Dusty. Frankie bawled because he was too young to go with us, but he stopped after Papa promised to take him next year.

The summer before Papa had got us lost on our camping and fishing trip. Mamma had to send Uncle Mark to find us. This year Papa decided to play it safe. We went to Beaver Canyon, where we'd gone fishing several times in the past. Beaver Creek, which ran down the canyon, was just the right size for trout fishing. It was larger than a stream but not big enough to be called a river. We didn't stop at the main campground but kept on going two miles up the canyon to a smaller campground.

After we'd made camp there was still time to get in some fishing before supper. Papa and Sweyn went fishing in the rapids of Beaver Creek. Sweyn caught four rainbow and two German brown trout. Papa, using his jointed bamboo rod and reel and fly hooks, caught three good-sized rainbow trout. Tom and I, using our poles and fishing from the bank of the creek, didn't even get a bite. And boy, oh, boy, did Sweyn pour salt in our wounds as we ate the trout for supper.

The next morning Sweyn and Papa again went fly-fishing in the rapids. Tom went upstream. I started fishing in a hole just below the rapids. I finally caught a rainbow trout. But it was only five inches long so I threw it back. And just as I did I heard Papa yelling.

"Don't let him get away, son!" Papa shouted.

I could see Sweyn had a huge trout on his line and it was giving him a heck of a fight.

"Don't let him get away!" Papa shouted again as he ran into the rapids in his hip boots, holding out his net.

"Don't help me!" Sweyn yelled.

I guess he didn't want Tom saying that he didn't land the big fish himself. But Papa couldn't have helped anyway. He slipped on a rock and fell into the water.

I grabbed my fishing pole and ran up the creek bank until I was opposite the rapids. Sweyn was still playing that big fish. Papa was on his feet, shouting encouragement. Slowly but surely Sweyn reeled in his line. But he had to battle that trout every inch of the way until he finally landed it in his net. He waded through the rapids to the bank of the creek. Papa sat down on the ground to empty the water out of his hip boots. Then he took the net and the huge, German brown trout from Sweyn.

"This has to be the biggest trout ever caught in Beaver Creek," Papa said, as proud as if he had caught the fish himself.

I had to agree with Papa. For my money Tom could kiss his three dollars and seventy cents good-by. We walked to camp and weighed the big trout. A two-pound trout was considered a good-sized fish for a mountain creek or stream. The German brown trout weighed three pounds and two ounces. Tom didn't return to camp until Papa started preparing our lunch.

"Hail the great fisherman!" Sweyn shouted.

"Didn't even get a bite," Tom said.

Sweyn showed him his German brown trout and made Tom check the weight.

"You haven't won yet," Tom said stubbornly.

I went with Tom after lunch. It didn't take me long to discover why he hadn't even gotten a bite. He wasn't fishing. He was exploring upstream. He picked up a long pole he'd cut from an aspen tree, and we walked upstream until we came to a fishing hole. Tom leaned over the bank and stuck his pole into the water.

"What in the heck are you trying to do?" I asked, as curious as all get out.

"I'm trying to find the deepest hole in the creek," he answered. "The deeper the hole the bigger the fish on the bottom. But I can tell you one thing, J. D. I believe all the deep holes upstream are pretty well fished out because they are closer to the main campground. Tomorrow I'll try downstream."

We were greeted with more jeers from Sweyn when we returned to camp for supper without any fish. After eating,

Tom said he was going to try some night fishing.

"Fish all day," Sweyn said, "and fish all night. But you'll never catch a fish as big as my German brown trout."

Tom was gone two hours. The next morning I went downstream with him. We walked about a mile and found three deep holes. When the sun hit the water just right, we could see some big trout on the bottom of two of those holes. But they sure as heck weren't biting. All we caught were a couple of little fellows we threw back.

Papa was a man who believed if you caught fish you had to eat them. We had trout again for lunch.

"I'm getting tired of eating trout," Sweyn said. "I think I'll go hunting this afternoon."

"See if you can get some quail or rabbits," Papa said.

After we had washed the tin plates, tin cups, and knives and forks in the creek, Sweyn went hunting. I went downstream with Tom. He entered an aspen grove and took out his jackknife.

"What are you going to do?" I asked.

"Make about six fishing poles and set them over those two deep holes we found," he said.

"Won't that be cheating?" I asked.

"I bet Sweyn that I'd catch the biggest fish with a pole, line, and hook and worm bait," Tom said, smiling. "I didn't say that I would use just one particular pole."

I helped him cut and trim six fishing poles and tie lines and hooks to them.

"What if Sweyn or Papa come downstream and see all these poles you've set?" I asked.

"I'm only going to set them at night," he answered. "Right now we'll hide them in the bushes."

63

We hid the poles. Then Tom put his arm around my shoulders.

"It is up to us," he said solemnly, "to save our brother from becoming a selfish person and a braggart."

Sweyn had as much luck hunting as he had fishing. He returned with four quail.

Papa looked at the birds. "We will have roast quail for supper," he said. "And I'm going to cook them the way trappers and mountain men cooked them. You boys cut off the heads and feet and clean the birds but leave the feathers on."

My brothers and I went down to the creek to do what Papa asked.

"Boy, oh, boy," I said, "if Papa thinks I'm going to eat quail with the feathers on them, he has got another think coming."

Sweyn shook his head. "He always gets some crazy idea from some book about trappers or mountain men he has read."

When we returned to camp, Papa stuffed the birds with Indian meal, pounded crackers, and plenty of salt and pepper. He let our campfire burn down to red embers. Then he placed the quail on red-hot coals and used our shovel to cover them with more hot coals and ashes. I lost my appetite from the smell of the burning feathers.

"Now, boys," Papa said proudly, "we will just let them cook for half an hour."

When the half hour was up Papa uncovered the birds. He got a fork and put one of the quail on a tin plate. He held the bird with the fork and peeled the skin and burnt feathers off as if they were paper. He placed one quail on each of our plates. I got my appetite back in a hurry. That was the tastiest and tenderest and best quail I'd ever eaten in my life.

"You can do the same thing," Papa told us, "with partridges, ducks, wild fowl, and fish. We must try it with some trout."

After the supper dishes were washed, Tom said he was going to do some night fishing. I went with him. Papa and Sweyn began playing casino with a deck of cards we'd brought along. I helped Tom get the six poles. We baited the hooks with worms and set the poles over the two deep holes where we'd seen big fish on the bottom. We put good-sized rocks on the handle end of the poles, in case we caught anything during the night.

"I'll get up early in the morning," Tom said, "and see what I've caught. If I don't get a bigger one than S. D. got, I'll use a fish lantern tomorrow night."

"What is that?" I asked.

"You'll see," he said. "Papa isn't the only one who read that book about trappers and mountain men."

When I woke up in the morning Tom was gone. Papa and Sweyn were just starting to get dressed. We came out of the tent just as Tom arrived. He had four good-sized trout but none of them anywhere near as big as the one Sweyn had caught.

"No wonder I couldn't catch any fish before," he said. "I've been fishing downstream and all the holes are fished out. But look at these beauties I caught this morning upstream."

I knew Tom had caught the trout on the poles we had set. I also knew why he'd said that he caught the fish upstream. He didn't want Sweyn going downstream. After breakfast Tom got his homemade wooden tackle box and I got mine. We walked upstream with our poles and tackle boxes until we came to the first deep hole.

"Darn it," Tom said, looking back. "Sweyn *would* decide not to fish the rapids today."

Sure enough, Sweyn was following us. He caught up with us and began casting over the deep hole.

"If you can catch four medium-sized trout with a pole and worms in this hole," he said, "I'll show you how to catch some big ones flyfishing."

I thought it strange that Tom didn't open his tackle box but asked me for some bait, even though I knew he had a whole can of worms. We baited our hooks and dropped our lines into the deep pool. Sweyn gave up in about an hour, after only catching a little six-inch rainbow. He went back to fishing in the rapids.

Tom opened his tackle box. "Keep a sharp lookout, J. D.," he said. "Let me know if Sweyn or Papa head this way."

I was so curious about what Tom was doing that it was hard for me to keep a sharp lookout. He removed a half-pint whiskey flask with the label washed off from his tackle box. It had some kind of liquid in it.

"What's in the flask?" I asked.

"Sweet oil I got from Mamma's kitchen," he answered.

Then he got an empty, clean, pork-and-bean can from his tackle box. He filled it half full of water from the stream. I watched wide-eyed as he took something wrapped in tin foil from the box. He unrolled the tin foil, revealing something white about the size of a marble.

"What is that?" I asked.

66

"A piece of phosphorus," he said as he dumped it into the can of water. "I had to tell Mr. Nicholson at the drugstore why I wanted it because it is poisonous."

Then he took out his jackknife and opened a blade. "It has to be cut under water," he said.

"Won't it dissolve?" I asked.

"Not in water," he answered. "But after I cut it into small pieces it will dissolve in the sweet oil."

He cut up the piece of phosphorus under water. Then he poured the water from the can. He used the tip of the knife blade to put the pieces of phosphorus into the whiskey flask. Then he put the cork in the bottle good and tight.

"And that, J. D.," he said, "is how trappers and mountain men made fish lanterns."

"I don't see any light coming from it," I said.

"It takes a few hours for the phosphorus to dissolve in the sweet oil," he explained. "I'm going to circle the camp and go hide the fish lantern with the poles."

It was lunchtime when Tom returned. During lunch Sweyn got in a few more digs at Tom. He had caught four good-sized trout that morning.

"I think you had better confine your fishing to before breakfast," he said to Tom. "That seems to be the only time you can catch anything."

"Maybe you are right," Tom said. "I think I'll go hunting this afternoon."

Papa nodded his head. "Try to get some more quail," he said. "They were delicious."

I went hunting with Tom. We didn't get any quail but we did kill three rabbits. We had fried rabbit, beans, and sourdough biscuits for supper. After eating Tom said he was going to go night fishing. I went with him. We started upstream and then circled the camp to get to where the poles and fish lantern were hidden. Tom dug up the whiskey flask from under ground, where he had buried it. And I'll be a four-legged duck if that flask wasn't shining as if it had a light inside it.

"How did you do it?" I asked.

"The sweet oil dissolves the phosphorus," he explained, "forming a thick fluid that throws out light."

"Now that you've got it, what are you going to do with it?" I asked.

"You'll see," he said.

We walked downstream to the deep pool where we had seen the big trout on the bottom. Tom removed the hook from one of the poles. He tied the end of the line around the neck of the flask. Then he tied a rock to the fishing line so it would sink in water. He lowered the fish lantern into the deep hole. It gave me the willies, seeing that eerie light under water.

"What's the idea?" I asked. "So the fish can see the bait at night?"

Tom laughed. "No, J. D.," he said. "According to the book, fish are attracted by any unusual brightness in a deep pool. When those big fellows on the bottom see the fish lantern they will come up to look at it. And when they do, they will see the bait. I am just hoping they will be hungry."

Tom put big fat worms on the hooks of four of the poles. He set the poles so a baited hook was on each side of the fish lantern.

I was positive when I went to bed that night that the fellow who wrote the book was telling a tall fish story. Tom woke me up with his hand over my mouth while it was still dark. We slipped out of the tent and dressed quietly. Taking our fishing poles and tackle boxes with us, we walked downstream to the deep hole. I could tell from the tightness on three lines there had to be fish on the other end. The sun was just coming up as Tom picked up the first pole.

"Got one," he said, grinning.

But he wasn't grinning for long after landing the fish. It was just a medium-sized rainbow trout. Tom removed the rock and picked up the second pole. I knew from the way he held it and the tightness of the line that he had a big one this time. He began to back up to keep the line tight. And suddenly the biggest trout I'd ever seen was stirring up the water in the pool.

"Don't lose him!" I shouted.

That fish gave Tom a longer and harder battle than the German brown had given Sweyn. But when Tom finally landed it, it was the biggest rainbow trout I'd ever seen. It was a beauty and had to outweigh Sweyn's by at least a pound. And I had to take my hat off to the fellow who wrote that book. Tom hauled in another rainbow trout bigger than Sweyn's on the next pole. The fourth pole didn't have a fish on the hook. But Tom had two big trout and either one of them would outweigh the trout Sweyn had caught.

"You did it!" I shouted. "And if that doesn't cure Sweyn of his selfishness and bragging, I don't know what will."

I removed all the hooks and lines from the poles while Tom took care of the fish lantern. We hid the poles and buried the fish lantern in the ground so it couldn't be seen at night. We circled the camp to make it appear we were coming from upstream. Tom had the three trout hooked through the mouth and gills to a Y tree branch. We hid in the bushes until we saw Papa and Sweyn come out of the tent.

"Now, J. D.," Tom said. "And don't forget to yell what I told you."

I ran from behind the bushes toward the campsite. "Papa!" I shouted. "Papa! Papa! Wait until you see what T. D. caught! Get the scale ready!"

Tom came from behind the bushes, holding up the three trout. Papa got so excited he ran to meet us. He took the fish from Tom.

"Get them in water," Papa said proudly. "We will want to take them home with us, packed in wet mud and grass to show people. There is no doubt about it. These are the biggest trout ever caught in Beaver Creek."

"Not until I weigh the biggest one," Tom said.

Papa insisted on weighing the biggest one himself. It weighed four pounds and five ounces. Poor Sweyn stood staring at the scales. He looked like a cowboy who, after losing his month's pay playing poker, comes out of a saloon and finds somebody has stolen his horse.

"I've still got all day," he said.

"Take all day," Tom said, grinning. "And take all night too. Just remember we are breaking camp and leaving for home in the morning right after breakfast."

Tom and I sure got even with Sweyn for his selfishness and bragging that day. Tom's trick of pretending he'd caught the fish upstream worked. Sweyn began fishing the deep holes upstream. Tom and I sat on the bank of the creek getting in our digs.

"You are wasting your time in this hole," Tom said. "It is all fished out."

"You are just trying to talk me out of fishing this hole," Sweyn said.

"Just be careful with my rod and reel," Tom said. "I don't want either one broken when you hand them over to me."

"I'll bet, T. D.," I said, "that you aren't going to be selfish like some fellow we know when the rod and reel belong to you."

"That is a bet you'd win," Tom said. "You can practice casting any time you want. And when we go on our fishing trip next year, you can use my rod when I go hunting."

I don't know if it was to get away from Tom and me or because he hadn't caught anything, but Sweyn finally decided to give up fishing the deep holes upstream. That afternoon he went back to fishing in the rapids. And for the first time he decided to try some night fishing after supper. Papa began to get a little edgy when Sweyn hadn't returned by nine o'clock.

"We had better go look for him," Papa said. "He might have slipped on a rock and fallen or something."

We found Sweyn upstream, fishing in the dark at one of the deep holes.

"I know this is our last day," Papa said, "but it is time we turned in."

I couldn't help feeling a little sorry for Sweyn when we got back to camp. He removed the reel and carefully placed it in its box. Then he unscrewed the rod and placed it in its canvas bag. But the saddest part of all was watching him remove the fly hooks from his fisherman's

72

hat and placing them in a box. Then he handed Tom the rod, the reel, and the fly hooks.

"You won the bet," he said sadly. "They're all yours now."

Papa stared at Sweyn over the flames of the campfire. "Just what was that all about?" he asked.

"I bet T. D. that I would catch the biggest fish on this trip," Sweyn answered.

Papa then turned his head and stared at Tom. "Knowing you as I do," he said, "I'm positive you wouldn't have made the bet unless you knew you would win. But for the life of me I can't understand how you could possibly know that you would catch the biggest trout."

"Fisherman's luck," Tom said, grinning. "And J. D. is my witness that I won fair and square. I caught both of those big trout using just a pole, line, hook, and worm bait."

"That's right, Papa," I said. "And T. D. only made the bet to cure Sweyn of his selfishness and bragging."

"What selfishness and bragging are you talking about?" Papa asked.

I told him how selfish Sweyn had been with his rod and reel and how he had boasted he would catch twice as many fish as Tom and me put together.

Papa was shaking his head when I finished as he looked at Sweyn. "Under the circumstances," he said, "you deserve to lose your fishing gear. Perhaps it was providence's way of punishing you for being selfish and a boaster. Let's go to bed now."

And that is the story of how The Great Brain hooked a fish named Sweyn.

CHAPTER FIVE

Alkali Flats

A FEW MILES SOUTH of Adenville there were twelve hundred and eighty acres of land called Alkali Flats which nobody wanted because it was all alkali soil. Being rather arid country, Utah has many of these large alkali beds. Nothing would grow on this land, not even range grass for grazing, which made it worthless. Papa told us an easterner named Boswell had bought the land sight unseen many years ago. When he discovered it was all alkali soil, he had stopped paying taxes on the land.

Every year old-man Hobbs, the country treasurer and tax collector, posted delinquent tax notices on Alkali Flats in Papa's newspaper. Anybody foolish enough to pay the back taxes could have the land.

It was right after we returned from our fishing trip that a man named Wilbur Cummings arrived in town. He registered at the Sheepmen's Hotel. He purchased a dozen fruit-canning jars at the Z. C. M. I. store. The full name of the store was Zion's Cooperative Mercantile Institute. There was one of these stores owned by the Mormon church in every town in Utah. The only thing Mr. Harmon, the manager of the store, found out about Mr. Cummings was that he was a chemical engineer.

Mr. Cummings rented a horse and buggy at the livery stable and drove out to Alkali Flats. He took samples of the alkali soil in twelve different places, putting the soil in the twelve fruit-canning jars. Upon his return he went to the courthouse where he was told Alkali Flats could be purchased for back taxes. This caused a lot of curiosity in town. But Mr. Cummings refused to answer any questions before leaving Adenville.

A few days later another stranger arrived on the morning train from Salt Lake City. He was a distinguished-looking gentleman with gray hair, a gray mustache and goatee, and he was wearing very fashionable clothes. He took the most expensive suite at the Sheepmen's Hotel and registered as Francis K. Pendleton from Chicago.

Mr. Pendleton went to the courthouse after eating lunch at the hotel. He purchased Alkali Flats in the name of Alkali Products Incorporated for two hundred and ten dollars in back taxes. Then he rented a horse and rig and drove out to the farm of Carl Underwood. He told the farmer he wanted an option to build a spur track from the railroad across the south pasture of his farm to Alkali Flats. He offered a hundred dollars for a thirty-day option to purchase the right-of-way for fifteen hundred dollars before the option expired. Mr. Underwood was delighted because he would have sold his whole farm for two thousand dollars. He rode into town with Mr. Pendleton. They went to the law office of Judge Potter, where the option papers were signed and the hundred dollars in cash given to Mr. Underwood.

The next morning Mr. Pendleton went to the telegraph office. He sent a telegram to Frederick Ames Hollingsworth, President, Alkali Products Incorporated, Salt Lake City branch office in the Newman Building. Nels Larson, who was the telegrapher, station master, and everything else at the depot, made a copy of the telegram.

Calvin Whitlock, the town mayor and president of the Adenville Bank was seated in his private office when Nels entered.

"I know it's against the rules," Nels said, "but I made a copy of a telegram I think you should see." He handed the copy to the banker. It read:

PROPERTY KNOWN HERE AS ALKALI FLATS IS NOW OWNED BY ALKALI PRODUCTS INCORPORATED. OPTION FOR SPUR TRACK RIGHT OF WAY THROUGH UNDERWOOD FARM HAS BEEN NEGOTIATED. ESTIMATE WE WILL NEED APPROXIMATELY FORTY THOUSAND DOLLARS TO BEGIN MINING OPERATION HERE. SUGGEST COMPANY RAISE NEEDED CAPITAL BY ISSUING ONE THOUSAND SHARES OF FIFTY DOLLAR PAR VALUE PREFERRED STOCK FOR SALE TO CHICAGO BROKERAGE HOUSES AT TEN PERCENT DISCOUNT. WILL ARRANGE FOR SURVEY OF PROPERTY TODAY.

FRANCIS K. PENDLETON
VICE PRESIDENT

Mr. Whitlock sent for Papa after reading the telegram.

"This is the biggest economic development that could happen to Adenville," he told Papa. "You and I are going to call on Mr. Pendleton and convince him that the citizens of Adenville should be permitted to buy stock in the company."

The banker telephoned the hotel. Mr. Pendleton wasn't in but Mr. Whitlock knew Robert Meredith was the only surveyor in town. He reached Mr. Pendleton in the surveyor's office. Mr. Pendleton told the banker he was going out to Alkali Flats with Mr. Meredith that morning but would meet Mr. Whitlock and Papa in his hotel suite at two o'clock.

Mr. Pendleton was such a high-class fellow that he didn't go to a barber shop for a haircut. Danny Forester's father was cutting Mr. Pendleton's hair in the suite when Mr. Whitlock and Papa arrived. The banker introduced himself and Papa.

"I assume, gentlemen," Mr. Pendleton said, "that you are here to learn why Alkali Products Incorporated purchased Alkali Flats. Our company manufactures lye, soap, and Epsom salts. Our present source of supply for raw material is getting low. We sent our chemical engineer, Mr. Cummings, west to locate a large bed of alkali soil rich in the chemicals needed for our products. With the help of state boards of agriculture Mr. Cummings located large alkali deposits in Kansas, Colorado, and Utah. But the others were either too far from a railroad or so poor in the chemicals needed as to be worthless."

"Excuse me," Mr. Forester said, as he moved Mr. Pendleton's head slightly to continue the haircut.

"To go on, gentlemen," Mr. Pendleton said. "One alkali bed suggested to Mr. Cummings was Alkali Flats. You will be glad to know that the soil is very rich in the chemicals needed for our products and only half a mile from the main railroad line. We expect to be mining and shipping carloads of raw material to our Chicago plant in about two months. We will employ approximately twenty-five local men when mining operations begin. I believe that answers all of your questions, gentlemen."

"Not quite," Mr. Whitlock said. "Mr. Larson showed us a copy of the telegram you sent."

At first Mr. Pendleton was angry. "Doesn't your Mr. Larson know that is against the rules and regulations?" he asked. "I could have the man terminated for it." Then he shrugged. "No real harm has been done. Whatever was in the telegram will become public knowledge when the new stock is issued."

"That is what we wanted to talk to you about," Mr. Whitlock said. "As mayor of Adenville, may I suggest that your company permit our citizens to invest in the first big industry to locate here?"

"I'm sorry," Mr. Pendleton said, "but that is impossible. The thousand shares of stock will be sold to stockbrokers in blocks of one hundred shares at forty-five dollars a share. This will enable the company to get the capital needed immediately. The brokers will then sell shares of stock to the public. You can purchase stock that way. Instead of paying forty-five dollars a share, the stock will cost you about fifty-five dollars a share. The brokerage firms must pay their salesmen a commission and make a profit. But even at fifty-five dollars a share the stock is a bargain. It will be worth a great deal more when we pay our first dividend in about six months."

Mr. Whitlock didn't become a banker because he didn't know his arithmetic. "Assume that other citizens and I," he said, "wanted to purchase a block of one hundred shares. Could we buy them at the same price as a stockbroker?"

Mr. Pendleton thought about it for a moment. "I can't think of any possible objection," he said. "I would, of course, have to get President Hollingsworth's approval. And I would have to be certain that the money to pay for the stock was on deposit in your bank."

"I see your point," Mr. Whitlock said. "Some people might say they want to buy shares and then change their minds at the last moment. But I can set up a special account in the bank to handle it."

Mr. Forester finally finished the haircut and left the suite with the first gratuity of his life. Mr. Pendleton gave him a fifty-cent tip.

"Now, gentlemen," Mr. Pendleton said, after putting on his frock coat and removing a business card from his wallet. He handed it to Mr. Whitlock. "Send me a telegram to our Salt Lake City branch office certifying you have the cash in a special account to purchase a hundred shares of stock."

"What if we want to purchase more than a hundred shares?" Mr. Whitlock asked.

"Let me know how many shares you want to purchase in the telegram," Mr. Pendleton said. "I will then take it up with Mr. Hollingsworth. But you do understand that the stock must be purchased in blocks of one hundred shares. And Mr. Fitzgerald, please don't print anything about this in your newspaper or notify the Salt Lake City papers. If it became known that our company was permitting the citizens of Adenville to buy the stock at forty-five dollars a share, we would be deluged with demands from investors to sell them stock at the same price."

Papa was certainly excited when he came home that evening. Before supper, during supper, and after supper, he talked about his visit with Mr. Pendleton.

Mamma let Papa ramble on until he said he was going to mortgage the house to buy stock.

"You will do no such thing," she said. "There are enough of the worthless stocks you've bought in a trunk in the attic to paper the walls of this parlor."

"But those were high-risk stocks, Tena," Papa protested, "with no guarantee that the companies would find gold or silver or oil on the property. This is a company that manufactures lye, soap, and Epsom salts."

"I have never seen the name Alkali Products Incorporated on any I've bought," Mamma said.

"That is because their market is in the central states," Papa said.

They were still arguing about it when the time came for Frankie and me to go to bed. Papa was a good talker but I knew Mamma would never let him mortgage the house. I stayed awake until Tom came up at nine.

"Papa could make us rich," I said, "if Mamma let him mortgage the house."

"Mamma knows that Papa doesn't know beans about stock," Tom said. "If Mr. Whitlock is going to invest, I just might buy a share of stock myself. I'm not a fellow who passes up a chance to almost double his money in six months. But I am also not a fellow who puts up forty-five dollars without knowing a lot more about Alkali Products Incorporated."

The next morning Tom went for a ride on Sweyn's mustang, Dusty. That afternoon he went to the post office to mail two letters and a mysterious package. I asked him what it was all about.

"Just protecting my forty-five dollars," he said, and that was all I could get out of him.

Mr. Forester didn't waste any time telling people what he had heard in the hotel suite. Everybody who could scrape up forty-five dollars or more was demanding that Mr. Whitlock let them buy shares of stock. The banker had his bookkeeper, Frank Collopy, record how many shares each person wanted to buy and made them deposit the money in the special account. Papa got a loan on the *Advocate* building to buy twenty shares of stock. Tom took forty-five dollars from his bank account to buy one share. The total amount of money deposited in the special account was enough to buy two hundred and twenty-one shares. Mr. Whitlock himself said he would purchase seventy-nine shares to bring the total up to three hundred.

He sent a telegram to Mr. Pendleton at the Salt Lake City branch office stating there was $13,500 in the special account—enough money to purchase three hundred shares. He received a telegram back stating that President Hollingsworth had approved the sale. Mr. Pendleton also requested that Mr. Whitlock mail him the name of each shareholder and the number of shares each person was buying. This was so the stock certificates could be issued in their names.

81

Tom went to the post office and opened our box every day. Finally, on Saturday, he received a letter from a boy he knew at the academy who lived in Salt Lake City. The letter read:

Dear Tom:

I went down to the Newman Building like you asked me to do. There was no Alkali Products Incorporated on the directory. I went up to the room number you gave me. It is just a place you can receive mail, telegrams, and phone calls by paying three dollars a month. Sure miss you and Tony and Jerry.

Your Friend,
Phil

I handed the letter back to Tom. "Does that make Mr. Pendleton a crook?" I asked.

"I'll need the answer to my other letter before I can convince Papa or anyone of that," Tom said.

The other letter arrived on Monday. It was from the State Board of Agriculture and read:

Dear Mr. Fitzgerald:

Our department has made a chemical analysis of the alkali soil you sent to us. The soil is unsuitable for the following reasons. There is not enough sodium hydroxide present to profitably manufacture lye or hard soap. There is not enough potassium hydroxide present to profitably manufacture soft soap. There is not enough magnesium sulfate present to profitably manufacture epsom salts. In short, this is a very poor grade of alkali soil for commercial purposes.

Yours truly,
Herbert Garrison

"I guess this proves Mr. Pendleton is a crook," Tom said. "Let's go tell Papa."

We ran all the way to the *Advocate* office. Papa and Sweyn were both setting type.

"Hold the front page for the biggest story of the year!" Tom shouted. "Mr. Pendleton is a confidence man."

Sweyn laughed a sort of dirty laugh. "It takes one to know one," he said.

"What nonsense is this?" Papa asked.

"There is no nonsense about it," Tom said. "I've got the proof that Mr. Pendleton is a crook." He handed Papa the two letters.

Papa read the letter from Tom's friend first and then handed it back. "It is a common practice," he said, "for a company to use a mailing and telephone service temporarily until they find a suitable location for a branch office."

"Read the other one," Tom said. "I'll bet that will convince you that Mr. Pendleton is a crook."

Papa read the letter from the department of agriculture. "Where did you get the sample of alkali soil you sent them?" he asked, as he handed the letter back to Tom.

"About twenty feet from the edge," Tom answered.

"That explains it," Papa said. "In as large a deposit of alkali soil as Alkali Flats, the chemical content is going to vary. And it stands to reason that the closer you get to the edge, the less alkali in the soil. That is why Mr. Cummings took samples in twelve different places."

"Then you don't believe Mr. Pendleton is a crook?" Tom asked, looking as flabbergasted as a rooster that has just laid an egg.

"I know you meant well, T. D.," Papa said, "but

please leave such business matters to me. Mr. Pendleton and the president of the company will arrive on the eleven o'clock train tomorrow morning. I don't want you showing or mentioning those two letters to a soul. I will not permit you to start an ugly rumor that might embarrass these two gentlemen."

Tom was plenty disgusted as we left the *Advocate* office. "It is easy to understand why Papa has a trunk filled with worthless stock in our attic," he said. "But I'm not going to let anybody give me a worthless stock certificate for my forty-five dollars. I'm going to see Uncle Mark."

"Papa said not to tell a soul," I said.

"I can't help what Papa said," Tom said. "Nobody is going to swindle me out of forty-five dollars."

We found Uncle Mark in his office, looking at wanted posters. The three jail cells were vacant.

"I think Mr. Pendleton is a crook," Tom said.

"So do I," Uncle Mark said, to our surprise. "But I've been through every wanted poster I have and can't find anything on him or that Cummings fellow."

"I've got the evidence to prove it," Tom said, handing Uncle Mark the two letters.

Our uncle was smiling after he read the letters. "You and your great brain have saved the people in this town thousands of dollars," he said. "I had a hunch Pendleton was a confidence man. Everything was just too pat—like having Mr. Forester give him a haircut in the suite. He knew the barber would tell everything he heard."

"Papa doesn't believe the man is a crook," Tom said. "I showed him the letters." Then he explained what Papa had said.

Uncle Mark looked worried. "If you couldn't convince your own father with this evidence," he said, "I would have one devil of a time trying to convince other citizens who want to invest."

"You could, if you proved there was no such company," Tom suggested.

"I thought of checking that out with the Chicago police," Uncle Mark said. "But I knew that if I were wrong, Nels Larson would tell it all over town and make me look like a fool. But with these two letters as evidence, I'm not worried about that any more."

We went with Uncle Mark to the depot where he sent a telegram to the chief of police in Chicago.

"Now, Nels," Uncle Mark said, "if you mention what is in that telegram or the reply I get, I am going to arrest you for revealing confidential information between two law enforcement officers. Is that understood?"

Mr. Larson nodded his head. He knew my uncle never made idle threats.

No reply had been received by the time the depot closed. The next morning Tom and I went to the depot. Uncle Mark was there waiting. It was almost ten o'clock before he got an answer to his telegram. He showed it to us. The telegram read:

MARK TRAINOR . . . MARSHAL . . . ADENVILLE, UTAH. IN REPLY TO YOUR TELEGRAM. NO ALKALI PRODUCTS INCORPORATED LISTED IN TELEPHONE BOOK, CITY DIRECTORY, BUSINESS DIRECTORY. NO RECORD OF A LICENSE EVER GRANTED THIS COMPANY AT CITY HALL.

> J. J. MALONEY
> CHIEF OF POLICE

I looked at Uncle Mark. "Are you going to arrest them when they get here on the eleven o'clock train?" I asked.

"No, John," he said. "We will let them sell their worthless stock first."

Calvin Whitlock, Papa, and all the leading citizens of Adenville were at the depot to meet the train. An elderly man wearing a plug hat, wing collar, cutaway coat, striped morning trousers, and pince-nez glasses got off the train with Mr. Pendleton and Mr. Cummings. Mr. Pendleton introduced the man as Frederick Ames Hollingsworth, the president of Alkali Products Incorporated. Then Mr. Hollingsworth made a short speech.

"Citizens of Adenville," he said in an oratorical voice, "it gives me great pleasure to permit some of you to become shareholders in our company. To those of you wanting a short-term gain, I can guarantee that the stock will be worth about seventy-five dollars a share in six months. To those of you wise enough to keep your stock, I can guarantee the market value will continue to increase and it will pay handsome dividends. My associates and I will register at the hotel and meet with Mr. Whitlock and the investors at the bank after lunch. Thank you."

There was applause and cheers from the crowd. When the three men arrived at the bank at one o'clock, a long line of investors was waiting. Mr. Pendleton was carrying a large briefcase. Mr. Whitlock had arranged two tables with chairs in the lobby of the bank. The three Alkali Products men sat at one table, Mr. Whitlock and his bookkeeper, Mr. Collopy, at the other table. Mr. Pendleton opened his brief case and removed a stack of stock certificates. He handed them to Mr. Collopy. The book-keeper added up the number of shares listed on the stock certificates on an adding machine. He told Mr. Whitlock that the total was three hundred shares. Then Mr. Whitlock went to the safe and returned with $13,500 to pay for the stock. Both Mr. Pendleton and Mr. Hollingsworth counted it. Then Mr. Pendleton put the money in the briefcase.

The line of investors then began filing by the tables. Each gave his name and the number of shares he had bought. Mr. Collopy hunted through the stack of stock certificates until he found the one belonging to each investor. Tom got in line and, after receiving his stock certificate, showed it to me. It was pretty fancy looking, with a green border. Tom's name and the figure "one" in a space in one corner and the word "one" on a line below Tom's name were all typed in. I thought for sure Uncle Mark would arrest the three men after everybody had received their stock certificates. But he didn't.

Mr. Hollingsworth went over to speak to Mr. Whitlock at his table.

"We will, of course," he said, "open a rather large checking account with you when we start operations here. Meanwhile, this money will be deposited in a Salt Lake City bank to pay for the construction of the spur track. I would appreciate it if you would keep the money in your vault overnight."

That last statement almost convinced me that Tom, Uncle Mark, and the chief of police of Chicago were all mistaken. I followed Uncle Mark and Tom outside.

"Why didn't you arrest them?" I asked.

"I want them to walk out of the bank with the

money," Uncle Mark said. "That will give me an air-tight case."

Tom and I left Uncle Mark and started walking home.

"If they are really crooks," I said, "why didn't they take the money and leave town?"

"Because there isn't a train out of here for Salt Lake City until tomorrow morning," Tom said. "And they know that if they rented horses at the livery stable it would attract suspicion."

"Why did they leave the money in the bank?" I asked. "Were they afraid of being robbed?"

"Heck, no," Tom said. "What better way to convince people they are just who they represent themselves to be than by leaving the money in the bank? That way they could leave town tomorrow and nobody would suspect they were confidence men for days or even weeks."

The next morning Tom and I were at the bank before it opened. Uncle Mark was already there. At five minutes to nine the three Alkali Products men arrived.

"Good morning, Marshal," Mr. Hollingsworth said. "What brings you here?"

"I just want to see you gentlemen safely on the train with the money," Uncle Mark said.

"Very commendable," Mr. Hollingsworth said.

Mr. Whitlock and Mr. Collopy were inside the bank. They opened the doors at nine sharp. The safe was opened and the briefcase containing the money given to Mr. Pendleton. The three men walked out of the bank with Uncle Mark following them. He waited until they were on the wooden sidewalk and then drew his Colt .45 revolver and pointed it at their backs.

"The jail is the other way, gentlemen," Uncle Mark said. "Just turn around and keep your hands in plain sight."

The three confidence men decided to plead guilty instead of having a jury trial. Judge Potter sentenced them to five years in prison. Tom was the star witness. And boy, oh, boy, was The Great Brain disappointed when Uncle Mark told him there was no reward for discovering that the three Alkali Products men were confidence men. He explained that a criminal just about had to rob a bank, a train, a stagecoach, or rustle cattle or commit murder before a reward was offered. But that disappointment was nothing compared to how Tom felt when he found that the citizens of Adenville weren't going to give him a reward either.

The only thing Tom got out of it was what they called a citation, which was issued by Mayor Whitlock and the town council. It was a letter signed by the mayor and city councilmen, praising Tom for meritorious achievement as a Junior Citizen of Adenville. I thought Tom was going crazy when he framed the citation and hung it on the wall in our bedroom. The first thing he did when he got up every morning was to stand and stare at that citation.

"You'll go plumb loco staring at that thing," I said one morning.

"I want it where I can see it every day to remind me of something," he said.

"Like what?" I asked.

"Yeah, what?" Frankie said.

"To remind me never to use my great brain to save

90

the citizens of this town," Tom said, "unless they give me a cash reward in advance."

"I wonder why they didn't give you a reward," I said.

"I wondered about it so much that I put my great brain to work on it," Tom said. "I figure they knew if they did give me a reward that it would be the same as admitting a kid was a lot smarter than them. And that is one thing no grownup will ever admit."

I knew the real reason Tom had investigated Alkali Products Incorporated was to protect his own forty-five dollars. I was going to remind him of that but changed my mind and here is why. I knew his money-loving heart was breaking because he didn't get a reward. I thought about my basketball and backstop and all the other things The Great Brain had swindled me out of. And I decided to let his money-loving heart go right on grieving. It would serve him right.

CHAPTER SIX

The Runaway

FRANKIE HAD NEVER been punished by Papa and Mamma until right after the Alkali Flats swindle. I don't know what got into him, but all of a sudden he became very mischievous. It began one evening during supper. Frankie liked jam on his bread instead of butter. Mamma had jelly on the table but no jam.

"I want jam," Frankie said.

"I just might have gotten you some," Mamma said, "if you had said please. Now you can either use butter or jelly on your bread."

Frankie picked up the bowl of jelly and turned it upside down on the table. We all couldn't have been more surprised if he had suddenly turned into a frog.

"Just for that," Mamma said, "there will be no dessert for you tonight, young man."

The next morning Eddie Huddle came over to play with Frankie. They began playing tag and chasing each other. Frankie knew he wasn't supposed to play in Mamma's flower garden. But he and Eddie started chasing each other around inside the flower garden and trampled down some of Mamma's prize flowers. She gave him a good tongue lashing.

Just before lunch it began to rain. Mamma phoned Mrs. Huddle to say that Eddie would have lunch with us on account of the rain. It was still pouring when we finished eating. Mamma told Frankie and Eddie to play either inside the house or on the back porch. They went to the back porch but didn't say there long. They took off their shoes and stockings and went wading in the rain puddles in the backyard. I guess they got tired of doing this and decided to have a mud-ball fight instead.

Mamma heard them yelling and went to the back porch. And what a sight she saw! Frankie and Eddie were making mud balls and throwing them at each other. They were both covered with mud from head to toe. Mamma made Frankie take a bath and go to bed. She cleaned up Eddie the best she could and told me to take him home. I guess Frankie thought taking a bath and having to go to bed in the afternoon was all the punishment he would get. But when Papa came home, Mamma told him what Frankie had done.

"I dislike doing it," she said, "but the boy must be punished."

She got Frankie out of bed, dressed him, and brought him into the parlor.

"Frankie," Papa said, "you know you weren't supposed to play in Mamma's flower garden and ruin her pretty flowers. You were told not to leave the back porch and you disobeyed. When a boy does things his parents have forbidden him to do, he must be punished. You will be given the silent treatment for one week."

I'd always figured the other kids in town were lucky. When they did something wrong they got a whipping and that was the end of it. But not the kids in our family. We got the silent treatment instead. This meant Papa and Mamma wouldn't speak to us. To me it was a lot worse than a whipping, which only lasted a few minutes.

Frankie had never received the silent treatment so I explained it to him. But he just didn't seem to understand. During our supper of fried pork chops and fried potatoes he asked Papa to pass the salt. Papa handed the salt shaker to Mamma who gave it to Aunt Bertha who passed it to Sweyn who finally passed it to Frankie. During the meal Frankie tried several times to get Papa and Mamma to speak to him. They pretended they didn't hear him.

Papa had always let Frankie blow out the match after he lit his after-dinner cigar. After supper Frankie stood by Papa's chair in the parlor waiting to blow out the match. But Papa blew it out himself.

"Why didn't you let me blow out the match?" Frankie asked.

Papa picked up a magazine and started to read. Frankie tried to climb up on his lap.

"J. D.," Papa said to me, "tell Frankie that he is not

94

to blow out the match, and he is not to sit on my lap, and he is not to speak to me for one week."

That was the system Papa and Mamma used to give orders when one of us was being punished. I walked over and took Frankie's hand.

"Don't bother Papa," I said. "Come on and play checkers with me."

I led him over by the fireplace and tried to get him to play checkers, but he just shook his head. He just sat there until Mamma and Aunt Bertha came into the parlor after finishing the supper dishes. Frankie got up. He waited until Mamma was seated in her maple rocker and had resumed working on a doily she was crocheting. He walked over to her.

"What are you doing, Mamma?" he asked.

She ignored him and spoke to Aunt Bertha instead. "Whose turn is it to entertain the Ladies' Sewing Circle tomorrow, Bertha?" she asked.

"Elinor Taylor's," Aunt Bertha answered.

Then Frankie tried to climb up on Mamma's lap. She pushed him away and spoke to me.

"John D., tell Frankie that if he doesn't stop bothering me he will be sent to bed," she said.

Frankie backed away from Mamma. "You and Papa don't love me anymore," he cried, tears coming into his eyes. Then he ran upstairs to our room.

"Poor little fellow," Mamma said sadly. "But he must learn to obey."

I knew how Frankie must feel so I went up to our room. He was sitting on our bed, staring out the window.

"Get undressed and we'll have a pillow fight," I said.

"Nope," he said.

"Want me to get the checker board?" I asked. "We can play up here until it is bedtime."

"Nope," he said.

I sat down beside him and put my arm around his shoulders. "I know how you feel," I said. "I remember the first time I got the silent treatment. It only lasted one day but it seemed like a year."

"That proves Mamma and Papa don't love me anymore," he cried. "You only got one day and I got a whole week."

I tried for about an hour to convince Frankie that Papa and Mamma loved him but he just wouldn't believe me. He cried himself to sleep that night.

The next day during breakfast and lunch he tried several times to get Papa and Mamma to speak to him. They both just ignored him. After lunch he went to the woodshed. I following him and found him crying. It was just too much. I went to the kitchen.

"Frankie is in the woodshed crying as if his heart is breaking," I told Mamma.

"It is breaking my heart to punish him," Mamma said. "But it must be done. If I let him get away with it this time, he will expect the same leniency next time. Little boys his age are quick to take advantage of any weakness they see in their parents. Aunt Bertha and I will be leaving for the Ladies' Sewing Circle in a little while. Keep an eye on Frankie and see he gets some cookies and a glass of milk this afternoon."

Tom and I tried to get Frankie to go swimming with us, but he refused to budge out of the woodshed.

"That means we can't go swimming either," Tom said. "Let's play some basketball."

"Not if you are going to charge me a penny to play," I said.

I guess Tom didn't want to play by himself so he let me play without charging me the usual fee. We played two-man basketball until about two o'clock when Frankie came out into the alley. He was pulling his wagon. His box of treasures that he kept in our bedroom was in the wagon. And so was his pup, Prince.

Tom stared at him. "Where do you think you are going?" he asked.

"I'm running away," Frankie said, "because Papa and Mamma don't love me anymore."

Tom winked at me. "Don't you think you had better have some milk and cookies first?" he asked.

"I guess so," Frankie said.

We all went to the kitchen where we had some oatmeal cookies and milk.

"I'll be going now," Frankie said as he got down from his chair.

Again Tom winked at me. "Where do you think you will go, Frankie?" he asked, just as serious as he could be.

"I'm not telling," Frankie said.

"If you don't want us to know," Tom said, "there is nothing we can do about it. But don't you think it would be a good idea to take along a sandwich?"

"I guess so," Frankie said.

Tom was really carrying a joke a long way. He actually made a ham sandwich and put it in a paper bag. We walked back to the alley. Frankie put the sandwich in his box. Prince had jumped out of the wagon. He put the pup back in it.

"Guess I'll be going now," he said.

97

"Good-by and good luck," Tom said.

Frankie picked up the handle of the wagon. "Good-by, John," he said.

"Good-by," I said.

"Good-by, Tom," Frankie said.

"Good-by," Tom said.

Frankie started up the alley. He went about ten feet and stopped and turned around.

"Good-by, John," he said.

"Good-by," I said.

"Good-by, Tom," Frankie said.

"We already said good-by once," Tom said. "So, for the last time, good-by."

We watched Frankie pulling the wagon down the alley with Prince sitting in it. He looked so pitiful it was actually comical. I couldn't help laughing and neither could Tom.

"I'll bet," I said, "that he turns around before he gets to the end of the alley."

"That is one bet I won't take," Tom said.

We were both wrong. Frankie kept going until he reached the street. He waved at us and then disappeared.

Tom sat down by the side of the woodshed and laughed so hard he had to hold his stomach. "He is hiding around the corner," he said, "waiting for us to come after him."

I sat down beside Tom and laughed too. But I stopped laughing after a few minutes when Frankie didn't return.

"Maybe we should go get him," I said.

"Remember that time you ran away from home when you were about his age?" Tom asked. "I sat right here and

watched you go up the alley, just like Frankie. I got worried when you didn't come back and went after you. And I found you playing with Jimmie Peterson in his backyard. Frankie will go to Eddie Huddle's home when he finds out we aren't coming after him."

"But Mamma said to keep an eye on him," I said.

"We know where he is," Tom said, "so what are you worrying about?"

We played basketball. Then we played catch until it was time for me to start doing the evening chores.

"I'll go get Frankie now," Tom said.

Mamma and Aunt Bertha returned just as I was filling up the woodbox in the kitchen. I began to get worried when Tom didn't return with Frankie by the time I'd finished all the chores. It was almost suppertime when Tom finally came down the alley. But Frankie wasn't with him.

"Where is Frankie?" I asked.

"I don't know," Tom said, looking plenty worried. "He wasn't with Eddie Huddle. I tried the homes of some other kids he plays with. No luck. I thought I could follow the tracks of the wagon but he must have pulled it in the street and the wheels didn't leave any marks on the gravel. Are you sure he didn't come back?"

"I'm sure," I said. "What do we do now?"

Tom took a deep breath. "We tell Mamma," he said.

Mamma was in the kitchen with Aunt Bertha preparing supper. Tom confessed that we had let Frankie run away and couldn't find him.

Mamma always reacted briskly in a crisis. "I'll deal with you two later," she said. Then she telephoned Papa and Uncle Mark. Supper was forgotten.

We were waiting in the parlor when Papa and Uncle Mark arrived. Tom told them what had happened. Uncle Mark stood up holding his Stetson hat in his hand.

"I don't think there is anything to worry about," he said. "A boy pulling a wagon with a dog in it is sure to be noticed. I'll check the houses on the street he took."

"I'll go with you," Papa said.

It was dark before Papa returned. Frankie wasn't with him. Mamma began to cry and so did Aunt Bertha. I sure as heck felt like crying.

"Please don't cry," Papa said. "Mark is organizing a search party. We did find one person who saw Frankie. Mrs. Cranston, who lives in that yellow house at the edge of town, saw him going down the road toward the river."

"The river!" Mamma cried. "Why didn't she stop him?"

"She assumed he was just taking his dog for a ride," Papa said. "T. D., get me the kerosene lantern from the barn."

I went to the barn with Tom.

"If anything happens to Frankie," I said, "I'll never forgive you."

"Forgive me?" Tom asked. "What about yourself?"

I knew Tom was right. I didn't have to go along with the joke. I could have stopped Frankie. I made a sacred vow never to play a joke on anybody again. As we started for the house Brownie began barking. In the moonlight I saw Prince come running down the alley. He had something in his mouth. When the pup got close enough, we could see it was the cap Frankie had been wearing. Tom put the lantern down and dropped to his knees.

"Good boy, Prince," he said, patting the pup on the head. Then he waved the cap in front of Prince. "Frankie," he said. "Take us to Frankie."

But Prince just wagged his tail.

"You try," Tom said.

I took the cap and waved it in front of Brownie's nose. My dog took the cap and dropped it in front of Prince and began barking. I think Brownie understood what we wanted, but the pup didn't. Prince just stood there, wagging his tail.

"There has to be a way," Tom said. "Take the lantern to Papa. But don't say anything about Prince. Too many people will just get the pup more excited."

I took the lantern to Papa. Then I went back to the alley.

"Did your great brain figure out how to make Prince take us to Frankie yet?" I asked.

"My great brain will make him understand," Tom said.

He took the cap and ran a few steps down the alley. "Frankie," Tom called. "Here, Prince. Find Frankie!"

The pup ran to Tom and he put the cap in the pup's mouth. But Prince just dropped the cap on the ground and stood there wagging his tail. Tom picked up the cap and ran a few more steps down the alley, calling to Prince. The pup followed him but stopped when Tom did.

"He thinks we are playing a game with him," Tom said as he walked back to where I was standing. "We know he loves Frankie. Just ignore him. Don't move or speak to him."

Then Tom threw the cap several feet down the alley. Prince ran to the cap and began to whine.

102

"Don't say anything," Tom whispered. "Just walk toward him."

We started walking toward the pup. Prince picked up the cap and ran down the alley. He turned around to see if we were following him. Then he began to run, with me and Tom and Brownie after him. He ran down the street Frankie had taken. When we got to the outskirts of town the pup turned around to see if we were still following him, then ran down the road leading to the river. He kept going for about a mile down the road. My lungs felt as if they were on fire. Prince turned off on a side road that led to a wooded glen where people often went for picnics. We found Frankie sitting with his back against a tree. Prince was licking tears from Frankie's face.

"John, Tom!" Frankie shouted, getting up and running toward us.

Tom reached him first and picked him up. "What a scare you gave us," he said.

"I was plenty scared when it got dark," Frankie said.

"We didn't think you would really run away," Tom said.

"I wouldn't have if it hadn't been for you and John," Frankie said.

I couldn't have been more astonished if Frankie had accused us of beating him. Tom was the first to recover from his astonishment.

"I thought you were running away because you didn't think Papa and Mamma loved you anymore," he said.

"That's right," Frankie said. "But I wasn't real honest sure until you and John didn't stop me. Then I knew that you both knew Papa and Mamma didn't love me anymore."

"Boy, oh, boy," I said to Tom. "When he tells Papa and Mamma that, you and I had better run away from home. They will never forgive us."

Tom put Frankie down. "Now listen," he said. "Papa and Mamma do love you. J. D. and I were just playing a joke on you."

"It's no joke," Frankie said, "to make me believe Papa and Mamma don't love me."

"We know that now," Tom said. "And we are sorry we played a joke on you. Now get into the wagon and sit on the box and we'll take you home."

Frankie was smiling as he got into the wagon. "It is good knowing I'm going home," he said. "And I won't tell that you and John played a joke on me."

We were on the river road, about a quarter of a mile from town, when we saw a group of men carrying lanterns coming toward us. I waited until they were near enough and then cupped my hands to my lips.

"Uncle Mark!" I shouted. "We found Frankie! He is all right!"

All the men with lanterns began running toward us. Papa and Uncle Mark reached us first. Papa picked up Frankie and hugged him.

"Are you all right, son?" he asked.

"I'm fine now that I know you love me," Frankie said as he put his arms around Papa's neck.

"Don't you ever forget how much I love you," Papa said, "and how much your mother loves you."

Papa carried Frankie all the way home. Tom told Uncle Mark and the other men in the search party how we had found Frankie. They left us at our front gate. I had never seen such a happy look on Mamma's face as when the three of us entered the parlor with Frankie.

"Give me my son," she cried. She took Frankie from Papa and sat down in her maple rocker holding him on her lap.

Frankie was struggling to keep his eyes open as Mamma rocked him in her arms. He fell asleep with a beautiful smile on his face.

Tom told Papa, Aunt Bertha, Mamma, and Sweyn how we had found Frankie.

"The worst part of it," Tom confessed, "was that Frankie was sure you really didn't love him when J. D. and I didn't try to stop him from running away."

Papa sat in his chair shaking his head. "You both played a very cruel joke on a little boy," he said. "It easily could have resulted in a tragedy. Frankie could have fallen into the river and been drowned. He could have wandered into that stretch of desert on the edge of town and been bitten by a rattlesnake. I can't imagine any punishment that is severe enough for what you two did."

"I can," Mamma said. "Just knowing what might have happened to Frankie will haunt both of you for the rest of your lives."

Mamma was sure right. My conscience gave me more punishment day and night than anything Papa could have done to me. Every time I looked at Frankie I couldn't help thinking he might have died as a result of a joke. I had terrible nightmares at night about finding Frankie dead. I told Tom about them.

"You aren't alone," Tom said, patting my shoulder. "But it is punishment we both deserve for playing such a joke on somebody we love."

CHAPTER SEVEN

The Magnetic Stick

I GUESS JUST ABOUT EVERY KID in town sort of envied Parley Benson. His father let him have things no other kid could have. Parley wore a coonskin cap just like Daniel Boone. When Parley was ten years old, his father gave him a genuine bowie knife. So it was no surprise to us kids when Parley's father gave him the first repeating air rifle ever seen in Adenville. Parley received the King air rifle for his birthday during the last week in July, right after Frankie had run away from home.

It was a beaut with barrel, handle, air chamber, plunger, piston, and all working parts made from brass and steel. It was so powerful it would shoot BB shot forty rods and kill rabbits and small game at fifty feet. It was the only repeating air rifle in town, and could shoot one hundred and fifty BB shots without reloading. Tom had a Daisy air rifle and I had a Quackenbush but we could only shoot one BB shot at a time.

Parley was showing off his air rifle to the kids at Smith's vacant lot the afternoon of his birthday. After demonstrating it, he told us he was going hunting. Every kid who owned an air rifle decided to go hunting with Parley, except Tom.

"Does that mean you'll look out for Frankie?" I asked.

"Yes," Tom answered.

I knew from the conniving look on The Great Brain's face why he wasn't going hunting. He was going to put his great brain to work on how to swindle Parley out of the King air rifle.

Tom was very quiet after supper that evening. He sat reading one of the books from our set of encyclopedias. Even Papa was impressed with how quiet Tom was.

"What are you reading that is so interesting?" he asked.

Tom looked up from the book. "I'm reading about Australia," he said. "We studied a little bit about the country in geography at the academy. But I want to know more about the aborigines."

"It is quite a country," Papa said. "It was originally settled as a penal colony by Great Britain. The aborigines are among the most primitive people in the world."

"I know all that," Tom said as if Papa had insulted his intelligence.

"Pardon me," Papa said. "I thought J. D. and Frankie might like to hear about it."

At any other time I would have liked to listen to Papa. But right then Frankie was going to beat me playing checkers if I didn't concentrate good and hard.

"Some other time, Papa," I said.

The next morning Tom disappeared. When he returned he was carrying what looked like a couple of branches from an oak tree. He took them up to his loft and pulled up the rope ladder. He wouldn't let me come up or tell me what he was doing. And after lunch I'll be a four-eyed bullfrog if he didn't take Papa's big, leather-bound dictionary, a rasp, and some sandpaper up to his loft. Tom stayed up in there all afternoon while Frankie and I went swimming. Tom also spent all the next day in his loft. The fellows at the swimming hole wanted to know if he was sick.

"Sick in the head," I said. "I don't know what he is doing but I'll try to find out tonight."

Tom was in the corral when Frankie and I arrived home. He showed us a bent piece of wood about a foot and a half long and sort of oval shaped.

"My great brain did it," he said. "The first one I made didn't work but this one does."

"What is it?" I asked.

"Something no kid or adult in this town has ever seen," Tom said. "It's a magnetic stick."

"You can't magnetize wood," I said.

"With a great brain, anything is possible," Tom said. "You'll find out tomorrow."

And that is all he would tell me until Frankie and I had finished the chores the next morning. He jumped down from the top rail of the corral fence.

"Go to Smith's vacant lot and round up the kids," he told me. "Tell them I've got a magnetic stick that I can throw in the air and make come back to me."

"Like fun I will," I said. "They will think you are crazy."

"And that, J. D.," he said, "is exactly what I want them to think. Just make sure Parley Benson is with you when you come back."

I was so curious that I figured it was worth letting the fellows think Tom was crazy. I rode my bike to Smith's vacant lot. Several kids were there, including Parley, batting fly balls and playing catch.

"I found out what Tom is doing," I said as they crowded around me. "He says he has made a magnetic stick that he can throw in the air and make come back to him."

Danny's left eyelid flipped open. "Nobody can magnetize wood," he said.

"Tom says his great brain did it," I said.

Seth Smith patted me sympathetically on the shoulder. "Pa always said that sooner or later people with great brains end up in the insane asylum," he said.

All the fellows wanted to see what a fellow bound for the insane asylum looked like. They accompanied me back to the corral. The minute I saw Tom I knew Seth was right. The Great Brain was standing in the corral, rubbing his bent piece of wood with a magnet. Then he took it in his right hand and threw it into the air, pointing the magnet in his left hand at it. The stick went spinning straight over the corral and then fell to the ground.

Parley shook his head. "He's gone plumb loco, for sure," he said.

109

Danny called out, "What are you doing, Tom?"

The Great Brain picked up the stick and walked over to the corral fence. "What does it look like I'm doing?" he asked with a wild look in his eyes. "I'm going to magnetize this stick so that when I throw it into the air and point a magnet at it the stick will return to me."

All the kids backed up a few steps. I didn't blame them. Nobody wanted to get too close to an insane kid. Seth pointed at Tom.

"You had better see a doctor," he said.

Parley nodded his head. "It's the booby hatch in Provo for you, for sure," he said.

"So you all think I'm crazy," Tom said. "I'll show you how crazy I am, Parley Benson. My great brain will figure out how to do it by one o'clock this afternoon. And I'll bet two dollars against your King air rifle that I can do it."

I was by now just as convinced as the other kids that Tom's great brain had blown a fuse. "Please don't bet him, Parley," I pleaded. "He doesn't know what he is saying or doing."

Danny slapped Parley on the back. "Go ahead and bet him," he said. "Tom used his great brain to swindle me out of my infielder's glove and to swindle you and every other kid in town. Now that his great brain is sick, we have a chance to get even."

"My great brain isn't sick," Tom said. "And I'm just as sane as any of you."

Parley stared at Tom. "They say an insane person will never admit he is crazy," he said. "I don't want to bet if you have gone insane."

110

"If I say I'm not insane," Tom said, "then you think I am insane. If I say I am insane does that mean you will believe that I'm sane? All right. I'm insane. Now go ahead and bet."

"Let me get this straight," Parley said. "You are betting two dollars cash against my air rifle that you can throw that stick in the air and make it come back to you. Right?"

"Right," Tom said. "I'll stand at one end of the corral and throw the magnetic stick. It will circle all around the corral and come back to me. If it doesn't, you win two dollars. If it does, I win the air rifle. Is it a bet?"

"It's a bet," Parley said. "Go ahead and show me."

"I need more time to magnetize the stick," Tom said. "Be here at one o'clock and bring the air rifle with you."

"I'll be here," Parley said.

I knew as I watched Parley and the other kids walk down the alley that Tom wasn't insane. I knew because any time The Great Brain bet two dollars in cash, he knew he was going to win the bet. But I started having doubts when Tom went to the woodshed and chopped up the stick.

"Why did you do that?" I asked.

"Yeah, why?" Frankie said.

"That was the first one I made," Tom said. "I didn't get it shaped right, and that is why it didn't work. But I've got one I made in the loft that does work."

"Do you mean your great brain figured out how to magnetize wood?" I asked.

"Of course not," Tom said. "I got the idea from reading about the aborigines in Australia. It's called a boomerang. I saw a picture of one in Papa's big dictionary. The aborigines use them to hunt. They can throw them hard enough to stun or kill small animals."

"How do the aborigines make the stick come back?" I asked.

"It is the way it is shaped," Tom explained. "The spinning motion creates air currents that bring a boomerang back to where it was thrown from."

"Then why all that mumbo jumbo about a magnetic stick?" I asked.

"That was a come-on to get Parley to bet," Tom said. "If I'd told the kids I could use a knife, rasp, and sandpaper to shape a piece of wood so it would return when thrown in the air, Parley and the other kids might believe it could be done. All the kids know you can't magnetize a piece of wood and that is why Parley bet me."

At one o'clock Parley and a dozen other kids came down the alley to our corral. Parley had his air rifle with him. Tom handed Seth Smith two dollars.

"You hold the stakes and be the judge, Seth," he said.

Parley handed Seth the air rifle. Then Tom went into the barn. He came out carrying a boomerang in his right hand and a magnet in his left hand. He rubbed the magnet against the boomerang for a couple of minutes. Then, holding the boomerang with his right hand, he threw it with a swift motion into the air. He pointed the magnet in his left hand toward the boomerang. The spinning boomerang made a circle in the air above the corral for about fifty feet. It came right back to where Tom was standing and dropped at his feet.

Tom had told me what a boomerang was and yet I sat there with my mouth open, unable to believe what I'd seen. The other kids stared at Tom as if The Great Brain were the devil himself.

Tom picked up the boomerang. "And just to prove it was no accident," he said, "I'll do it again."

He rubbed the magnet on the boomerang and then threw it into the air. He followed its circling motion with the magnet. The boomerang circled over our heads and again fell at Tom's feet. He picked it up and walked over to us.

"I guess that proves I'm not insane like you all thought," he said. "I'll take the two dollars and the air rifle now, Seth."

Parley jumped down from the railing. "Not until I make sure you used a piece of wood and not metal," he said.

Tom handed the boomerang to Parley, who examined it closely.

"It looks and feels like wood," Parley said, looking very disappointed.

"I'll prove it beyond a doubt," Tom said. He took the boomerang and tossed it into the water trough in our corral. "You can see it floats," he said.

"You win the bet," Parley said. "But the least you can do is give me the magnetic stick."

"It is no good now that it is wet," Tom said. "It cannot be magnetized again."

Seth handed over the two dollars and the air rifle. "I'll give you fifty cents to make one for me," he said.

Tom shook his head. "It takes a special kind of wood,"

he said, "and two days to make one. It wouldn't be worth it to me."

Danny touched Parley on the shoulder. "I'm sorry I talked you into betting," he said.

Parley was a good loser. "You didn't talk me into it," he said. "Let's go swimming."

I watched the fellows walk down the alley. "Teach me how to make boomerangs," I said to Tom. "I'm not a fellow who will pass up a chance to make fifty cents in two days. I'll bet I could sell one to every kid in town."

"If you started selling boomerangs," Tom said, "the kids would all say that I swindled Parley."

"They are going to say it anyway," I protested, "when their parents tell them you can't magnetize wood."

Tom picked up the boomerang from the water trough. "Nobody will ever be able to prove this piece of wood wasn't magnetized," he said.

And he sure as heck was right because he went into the woodshed and chopped up the boomerang. Then we went swimming with Frankie. I couldn't help feeling sorry for Parley as we sat on the sandy bank of the swimming hole. He told me that he would get the worst whipping of his life when his father returned from bounty hunting.

That made me begin to wonder about The Great Brain. Tom was the wealthiest kid in town. He had more money than some adults. He could have bought a King air rifle from Sears Roebuck and not even missed the money. But his money-loving heart wouldn't let him spend a penny for anything his great brain could get him for nothing. I had always been jealous of his great brain but I wasn't anymore. Parley was supposed to be Tom's friend. I knew that I would never do anything to make my good friends, Jimmie Peterson or Howard Kay, get the worst whippings of their lives.

CHAPTER EIGHT

The Good Raft Explorer

BY AUGUST OF THAT SUMMER I don't believe Tom had one real friend left in Adenville. None of them came over to play basketball anymore. They all seemed to be trying to avoid him. And there wasn't a kid left in town who would make a trade or a bet with The Great Brain. I sure as heck didn't blame them. After the swindles Tom had pulled off that summer, a fellow would have to have cabbages growing out of his head to bet or trade with The Great Brain.

But what the kids didn't know was that betting, trading, conniving, and swindling were to Tom what food and water was to them. I felt so sorry for Tom that I almost decided to let him swindle me out of something just so he could keep in practice.

We were sitting on the riverbank by the swimming hole one afternoon, keeping an eye on Frankie and Eddie Huddle. Tom looked like the fellow who lost his horse, his dog, and his best friend all at the same time.

"If I don't put my great brain to work on something," he complained, "it will start shriveling up."

"You sure as heck can't blame the fellows," I said. "When a kid sticks his head in a hole and gets whacked on the head with a club every time, he soon learns not to go around sticking his head in strange holes." I thought that was pretty darn clever but Tom didn't.

"There must be something I can put my great brain to work on and make some money," he said. "What would you like to do that you've never done before?"

"Fly like a bird," I said, quick as a flash.

"You know that is impossible," he said.

"I don't know about that," I said. "You've told me plenty of times that nothing is impossible with a great brain."

That night after supper I was sitting on the floor in the parlor reading *Huckleberry Finn* by Mark Twain to Frankie. Tom was studying the *World Almanac*. I was reading the part in the book about the trip down the river on the raft. Tom stopped reading and listened until it was time for Frankie and me to go to bed.

The next morning, while we were getting dressed, Tom asked me, "How would you like to go exploring on the river on a raft, like Huckleberry Finn?"

"Oh, boy," I said, "that would be a great adventure."

118

"Would you be willing to pay for it?" he asked.

"Sure," I answered. "How much would depend on how long the trip took."

"Say it took from half an hour to forty-five minutes," he said. "How much would you pay?"

"At least a nickel," I said. "Why?"

"I'm going to build a raft," he said, "and run exploring excursions on the river."

Eddie Huddle came over to play with Frankie just as the morning chores were finished. Tom saddled up Dusty and asked me if I wanted to take a ride with him. I got up behind him on the mustang. We rode to the swimming hole.

"I'll start the excursion on the raft from here," he said. "But now I have to find out how far downstream to go."

We rode Dusty along the riverbank until we came to the rapids. It was a place where the riverbed dropped, causing the current to flow swiftly. I pointed at the rapids.

"You will never get a raft upstream through those rapids," I said.

"I'll have to bring it back over land," he said. "Now to find a good landing place."

We rode until we came to a big bend in the river. Just around the bend the river became twice as wide and the current slow. We rode Dusty across the river and back to find out how deep it was. It was only about two feet deep all the way across.

"This will be the landing place," Tom said. "I figure the trip from the swimming hole to here on a raft would take about half an hour."

We returned home for lunch. After eating, Tom harnessed up the mare of our team.

"What are you going to do with Bess?" I asked.

"I need her to pull logs for my raft," Tom answered.

"Can I go with you?" I asked.

"Not unless you want to work," he said.

"How much will you pay me to help you build the raft?" I asked.

"Pay you?" Tom said as if I'd insulted him. "I am giving you a chance to learn how to build a raft and you want to be paid. You must have cockroaches in your head. I can get any kid in town to help me for nothing."

I sure as heck didn't want to lose out on learning how to build a raft. Someday I might be lost in the mountains and the only way to save myself would be to build a raft and float downstream to civilization.

"You don't have to pay me," I said. "But we can't leave Frankie alone."

"We'll take him with us," Tom said.

We got the two-man saw, the hand saw, and a tow chain from the toolshed and the ax from the woodshed. We rode Bess to Cedar Ridge, on the outskirts of town. It got its name from the cedar trees growing there. But there were also a lot of pine and aspen trees.

Tom picked out a young pine tree that had a trunk about eight inches thick. He cut a notch with the ax on one side to make it fall the way he wanted. Then we started sawing on the other side with the two-man saw. It was hard work, but I pretended I was a lumberjack and that made it fun.

"Timber!" Frankie shouted as the tree began to topple and then fell to the ground.

We cut off the top with the saw and then trimmed all the branches off with the hand saw and ax. When we finished we had a log about twelve feet long.

"We will need three more the same size," Tom said.

He hooked one end of the chain around one end of the log and the other end of the chain to tugs on Bess's harness. Bess pulled the log to our corral, with the three of us riding her. Frankie and I got off. Tom rode Bess inside the barn, pulling the log.

It took the next two days to get three more logs the same size and cut them in two. Tom laid the eight logs side by side on the ground in the barn.

"When we finish," he said, "I'll have a raft about five feet wide and six feet long."

"How did you learn how to build a raft?" I asked because nobody in Adenville had a raft.

"Out of Papa's book," Tom said. "Mountain men and trappers used vines or strips of animal skin to bind the logs together in the old days. I'll have to use rope instead."

It was now time for The Great Brain to part with some cash. For Tom this was like a soldier going to war parting from his sweetheart. And, oh, how it must have broken his money-loving heart to part with one dollar to buy fifty feet of rope. We returned to the barn with the rope. I helped Tom bind the logs together. We used slip-knots to tie the logs together about a foot from each end.

"Get a bucket of water from the water trough and soak the ropes," Tom said.

"Why?" I asked.

"To shrink the rope and make it good and tight," Tom answered.

We soaked the rope and then took Frankie's wagon and went to the lumberyard. Tom asked Mr. Hoffman if he had any scrap lumber.

"Going to build a doghouse?" Mr. Hoffman asked, probably because Brownie and Prince were with us.

"No, sir," Tom said. "I'm building a raft. I want to put a deck on the logs."

"How big is it?" Mr. Hoffman asked.

"About six feet long and five feet wide," Tom answered.

"You should have a solid board across the front and the rear," Mr. Hoffman said. "Then you can use scrap lumber for the rest of the deck."

"I wasn't figuring on paying for any lumber," Tom said. "Maybe Mr. Harmon at the Z. C. M. I. store has some old wooden crates he will give me."

"Who said anything about paying?" Mr. Hoffman asked.

He gave Tom two boards a foot wide and five feet long and more than enough scrap lumber for the deck. And I'll be the son of a sailor if he didn't give Tom a pound of nails free of charge too.

We returned to the barn. It was a good thing Tom had put the ropes binding the logs together a foot from each end. The two boards Mr. Hoffman gave him fit perfectly. We nailed them first. Then we used pieces of scrap lumber to finish the deck.

Tom stepped back to admire the raft. "All I need now is an oar and a oarlock," he said.

"What is an oarlock?" Frankie asked.

"It is a thing shaped like a horseshoe with a bolt on

122

the end," Tom said. "I'll show you a picture of one in Papa's big dictionary."

The next morning Tom took the dictionary with him when we went to the blacksmith shop owned by Eddie Huddle's father. Mr. Huddle was the strongest man in town. He was wearing his leather apron and shaping a red-hot horseshoe on his anvil when we arrived. We waited until he had shaped the horseshoe and, using his tongs, dunked it into the barrel of water to temper the steel.

Tom showed Mr. Huddle the picture of the oarlock in the dictionary. "I want you to make an oarlock like this one for me," he said. "I figure you can use a horseshoe and forge a bolt to the bottom of it."

"Why do you want it?" Mr. Huddle asked.

"For my raft," Tom said. "But first, how much will it cost me?"

"Not a thing, Tom," Mr. Huddle answered.

The blacksmith put a horseshoe and a bolt on his forge. Tom turned the handle on the blower of the forge until the metal was red hot. Mr. Huddle used his tongs, blacksmith's hammer, and anvil to forge the two pieces of metal together. Then he dunked the oarlock into the barrel of water to temper the steel. Tom thanked him and we started for home.

"One thing I can't figure out," I said. "Why did Mr. Hoffman give you the lumber and nails for nothing and Mr. Huddle make the oarlock free of charge?"

"Because they have guilty consciences," Tom said. "Both of them would have lost money in the Alkali Flats swindle if it hadn't been for me. And if they had tried to charge me, I was going to remind them of it."

"But you had to pay for the rope," I said.

"Because Mr. Harmon at the Z. C. M. I. store didn't invest in Alkali Products Incorporated," Tom said.

Tom got Papa's brace and a one-inch wooden bit from the toolshed. He drilled a hole near the center of the rear end of the raft. He put the bolt part of the oarlock into the hole in the deck board and log. He twisted the horseshoe back and forth.

"Now for the oar," he said.

I watched him make an oar out of an old pitchfork handle and a piece of board about six inches wide and a foot long. I didn't understand how the oarlock worked until he put the handle in the horseshoe part.

"Get the idea, J. D.?" he said as he moved the handle back and forth in the oarlock. "The oarlock does two things. It holds the handle of the oar and gives me the leverage needed to steer the raft."

"It's a beaut," I said. "Now all you've got to do is to figure out how to get the raft to the river."

"My great brain figured that out before I started," he said. "I knew I couldn't drag the raft over land or it would wear out the ropes around the logs. I'm going to use our stone sled to haul it."

Almost every family in Adenville had a stone sled. They were used instead of a wagon for small hauling jobs. We used ours every fall to haul manure to put on our vegetable and flower gardens and front lawn. The early pioneers used them mostly for hauling stones to build fireplaces. That is how they got their name.

Tom had told Papa that he was building a raft in the barn. During lunch he let Papa know the raft was completed.

124

"I'd better take a look at it," Papa said, "if you intend sailing it on the river."

Papa inspected the raft after lunch and pronounced it seaworthy.

"Now, J. D.," Tom said, after Papa had left the barn, "I want you to round up all the kids you can and tell them that they can get to see the first river-going raft ever built in Adenville. And all it will cost them is two cents."

"So that's why you didn't want anybody to know you were building a raft," I said. "But they will get to see it for nothing when you take it down to the river."

"Don't mention anything about me taking the raft to the river," Tom said. "Just tell them they get to see the raft and that's all."

Then Tom put his arm around my shoulders. "I've decided to make you a ten percent partner in this business venture," he said generously. "Your job will be to ride Bess, pulling the stone sled down to the landing place and hauling the raft back upstream to the swimming hole. You get ten percent of all the money I collect for fares. Of course, you can't expect ten percent of the money I get for showing the raft to the kids the first time."

"Shake on it," I said quickly. This was one time I was positive there was no way I could possibly lose making a deal with The Great Brain.

We shook hands. Then I rode my bike to Smith's vacant lot. The kids usually gathered there to play while waiting an hour after lunch to go swimming. A couple of kids in town had almost drowned from cramps because they went swimming right after eating. There were about a dozen kids there already. I told them about the raft. Those who didn't have any money with them went home to get some. Another bunch of kids showed up. I told them about the raft. News travels fast in a small town. I waited about half an hour but no more kids arrived. I found out the reason when I entered the barn. There were about fifty kids in our barn. But none of them had seen the raft yet. Tom had it covered with a horse blanket.

"I guess everybody is here," I told Tom.

He walked over and took hold of one corner of the horse blanket. Then, with a dramatic movement, he threw back the blanket revealing the raft. I'd never seen such a bunch of bug-eyed kids in my life.

"Behold the good raft Explorer!" Tom shouted. "The first river-going raft ever built in Adenville!"

Danny Forester's left eyelid was wide open as he stared at Tom. "Are you going to sail it on the river?" he asked.

"There will be morning and afternoon trips down the river," Tom said. "For a mere five cents you get to go exploring on a raft just like Huckleberry Finn. The trip includes shooting the rapids. Never before in the history of Adenville has such a thrilling, exciting, and dangerous adventure been offered to the kids in this town. The first trip will be this afternoon, starting at the swimming hole."

Then he picked up the coil of left-over rope. "Basil," he said, "you and Parley and Danny hold up one end of the Explorer."

I watched Tom loop the rope around the middle of the raft as the three boys held up one end. He tied a good strong knot in it.

"In case you are wondering," he said, "the rope is for the smaller kids to hold onto when we shoot the rapids."

I helped Tom hitch up Bess to the stone sled. The raft was lifted onto the sled. I got on Bess. Tom led the way out of the barn. When we reached the street a lot of adults stared at us. I guess they had never seen a raft being hauled on a stone sled with about fifty kids following behind.

When we arrived at the swimming hole, Tom stripped except for an old pair of pants.

"Line up, fellows," he said, "for the maiden voyage of the good raft Explorer. The fare is just a nickel, the twentieth part of a dollar, for the greatest thrill of your lifetime."

Every kid there wanted to go on the maiden voyage. There would have been a dozen fistfights over it if Tom hadn't solved the problem.

"We will go by your birthdays, beginning in January," he said.

Howard Kay was the only one born in January. Danny and Basil were born in February. Nobody had been born in March. Pete Kyle and Hal Evans were born in April.

"That is all for the first trip," Tom said, "because I have to take Frankie and only six passengers can go at a time."

The raft was carried into shallow water, and everyone climbed on board.

"You sit down, Frankie," Tom ordered, "and hold onto the rope."

Tom used the oar to push the raft into deeper water. Then he put the oar in the oarlock as the current began carrying the raft downstream. I got on Bess and began pulling the stone sled downstream. The kids who had been left behind ran with me, waving and yelling at the

passengers on the raft. I was surprised at how well Tom could steer the raft with his oar and oarlock. He kept the bow pointed downstream and the raft right in the middle of the river's current. The raft picked up speed as it neared the rapids. Tom ordered the five paying passengers to sit down. But he remained standing, holding the handle of the oar.

"Man the braces!" Tom shouted as the raft entered the rapids. "Man the top sail!"

The raft bounced up and down, dousing everybody on board with water but Tom remained standing. Tom wasn't fooling when he had promised his customers the thrill of a lifetime. The passengers were screaming and yelling like I'd never heard kids do before. And the kids running along the bank were carrying on as if they, too, were shooting the rapids. This was one time The Great Brain was giving the kids more than their money's worth.

There was a big bend in the river below the rapids. I left the bank of the river and took a shortcut. I got Bess to the landing place just as the raft came around the bend. When it was opposite me, Tom cupped one hand to his mouth.

"Ahoy the shore!" he shouted.

I hadn't expected this. I cupped my hands to my mouth.

"Ahoy the raft!" I shouted.

"The good raft Explorer asking permission to come ashore!" Tom shouted.

"Permission granted!" I shouted.

Then Tom and all the passengers except Frankie jumped off the raft. They waded through the two-feet-deep water and pushed the raft to the riverbank.

Danny was so excited it looked as if his left eyelid would never be half closed again. "Thought we were a goner in those rapids, Captain," he said to Tom.

"It was a mighty rough sea, Matey," Tom said. "But the good raft Explorer weathered it well." Then he looked at the kids who had run along the riverbank. "These land-lubbers don't know what they missed."

The trip downstream had lasted about half an hour. It took a little longer to haul the raft back to the swimming hole. Tom said there was time for one more trip.

"How about me?" I asked.

Tom hesitated and then looked at Basil. "You ride Bess down to the landing place," he said, "and take Frankie with you."

Then he collected five cents from each of the next five passengers and the Explorer was off on its second voyage.

It had been very exciting for me just watching the raft from the riverbank. But actually riding on it was the greatest thrill of my life. And Tom made it even more thrilling.

"Shiver my timbers!" he shouted as we entered the rapids. "By the Great Horn Spoon we are heading into a typhoon. Man the braces and hang on, men!"

And as we went through the rapids, I imagined I was standing on the bridge of my own ship in a raging typhoon.

After the second trip it was time for everybody to go home to do the evening chores. I rode Bess with Frankie as the mare pulled the raft to our barn.

"Why didn't you just leave the raft at the swimming

hole?" I asked Tom as we entered the barn.

"And have some kids get up early in the morning and go for a free ride?" Tom asked as if I were the stupidest person he'd ever met. "I figure I can make one trip in the morning and two in the afternoon every day except Sunday. Papa and Mamma wouldn't stand for it on Sundays. Six kids three times a day for six days out of the week comes to five dollars and forty cents I'll collect in fares. I hope you appreciate, J. D., that my great brain is going to make a fortune for you."

"I appreciate it," I said, and meant it.

Tom handed me a nickel. "I collected fifty cents in fares today," he said. "Here is your ten percent commission."

We unharnessed Bess. Then Tom sat on the railing of the corral fence while Frankie and I did the chores. He jumped down after we'd finished.

"You know, J. D.," he said, putting an arm around my shoulder. "I've been thinking. I'll be leaving for the academy in about three weeks. The weather here in Adenville is so mild you can run excursions on the river on Saturdays after school starts, at least during September and October. You could make ninety cents every Saturday if you owned the Explorer."

"Are you going to give me the raft?" I asked.

"Of course not," Tom said. "But I'll make you a business proposition. You give me a dollar to pay for the rope I bought. And also your ten percent commission on fares until I leave and I'll turn the Explorer over to you when I go back to the academy."

I knew from some sad experiences that it always pays to think twice when making a deal with The Great Brain.

"I'll think it over," I said.

"What's to think about?" Tom asked as if I'd insulted him. "During the next three weeks your ten percent commission will amount to a dollar and sixty-two cents. The dollar for the rope brings this up to two dollars and sixty-two cents. There are nine Saturdays in September and October. You would make ninety cents on each Saturday. That would amount to eight dollars and ten cents. Forget it, J. D. I'll sell the Explorer to some kid who isn't so dumb when it comes to figuring money."

I sure as heck didn't want to be known as a kid so dumb he didn't know the difference between two dollars and sixty-two cents and eight dollars and ten cents.

"Don't do that," I said. "I'll buy the raft from you."

"Shake on it," he said.

We shook hands to seal the bargain.

"And now, J. D.," Tom said, "it is always best to settle a business deal as quickly as possible. Let's go up to our room so you can get the dollar from your bank."

We went up to the room. I shook a dollar's worth of change out of my piggy bank and handed it to Tom.

"You are a nickel short," he said.

I stared at the money in his hand. "How do you figure that?" I asked. "Two quarters, four dimes, and two nickels make one dollar."

"You are forgetting the five cents commission I paid you today," Tom said. "Our deal was for a dollar plus all of your ten percent commission until I leave for the academy."

The Great Brain was right. I handed him another five cents.

CHAPTER NINE

The Wreck of the Explorer

PIGGY BANKS IN ADENVILLE sure took a beating during the next several days. The Explorer did a land-office business. Tom collected fares in advance every morning from the eighteen kids who would make the trip down the river, six at a time. He made more than thirty cents on some of these trips. Parley Benson, Seth Smith, Danny Forester, and other older boys wanted to be captain and pilot the raft down the river. Tom let them be captain and handle the oar and oarlock for an extra five cents. Some of the kids were making one trip almost every day. The Great Brain was making a fortune.

Every kid in town who had read *Treasure Island* by

Robert Louis Stevenson was now trying to talk like a sailor. They called each other "Matey" and the most popular song for kids was "Fifteen Men on the Dead Man's Chest, Yo-Ho-Ho, and a Bottle of Rum."

Then came that unforgettable Monday. I could see that it was raining in the mountains when I got up. But not one drop of rain fell in Adenville all that day. The Explorer made a trip down the river in the morning and another trip during the early afternoon. I was riding Bess, pulling the raft back upstream for the second trip of the afternoon. It was still raining in the mountains and it looked as if there was a real cloudburst up there. By the time I reached the swimming hole, the water in the river was getting muddy.

All the kids knew that when it rained in the mountains and the river water started turning muddy, there might be a flood. We always stopped swimming then. I was surprised when Tom had the raft carried back into the shallow water. I jumped off Bess.

"You can't make another trip," I told him. "The water is turning muddy and there might be a flood."

"Keep your mouth shut," Tom said. "I'm not about to pass up thirty cents because the water is turning a little muddy. The river has turned muddy before and there hasn't been any flood."

Jimmie Peterson and Howard Kay were passengers on the trip.

"To heck with you," I said to Tom. I walked over to Jimmie and Howard. "Don't go," I said. "There might be a flood."

Tom gave me a nasty look. Then he spoke to the passengers. "Anybody who is afraid of a little muddy water doesn't have to make the trip," he said. "But the Explorer sails on schedule. And no passage money will be refunded. All passengers who aren't fraidy-cats get on board."

After that speech all the passengers had to get on board or admit they were cowards. I got on Bess with Frankie and started downstream. Tom and his six passengers began the trip down the river. They were about a hundred yards past the swimming hole when I heard a roaring sound. I could see up the river for about a quarter of a mile, but I saw no sign of a flood and assumed what I'd heard was thunder in the mountains.

The raft reached that part of the river near the rapids where the current became swifter. I knew that the roaring sound wasn't thunder as it became much louder. I turned and looked up the river. A wall of angry, muddy water a couple of feet high was roaring toward me, carrying logs, uprooted trees, and debris. All the kids on the riverbank screamed for Tom and the passengers to get off the raft. Larry Hanson, Frank Jensen, Hal Evans, and Pete Kyle dove off and began swimming toward shore. They all reached it in time.

Tom was trying to get Jimmie and Howard to dive into the river before the flood reached the raft. But my two friends were too paralyzed with fright to move. I watched Tom wrap his legs around Jimmie with a scissor hold. Then he put his arms around Howard and grabbed hold of the rope on the raft. He was just in time. The wall of floodwater hit the raft and all three of them went out of sight for a moment before the raft bobbed back up to the surface.

I jumped off Bess and unhitched the stone sled. I

mounted her with Frankie behind me and made her gallop downstream. The raft hit the rapids and was tossed about as if it were a matchstick. Uprooted trees and logs smashed into it. A second wall of floodwater, almost three feet high, came roaring down the river and hit the raft right in the middle of the rapids. I couldn't see Tom, Jimmie, Howard, or the raft for what seemed like an eternity. Then the Explorer shot up to the surface as if tossed by a giant hand. The three boys were still on it. The raft spun crazily around, under water one moment and above water the next. The flood was carrying it downstream so fast that I couldn't keep up with it on Bess. The raft, Tom, and my two best friends disappeared in the raging water.

Frankie tightened his arms around my stomach. "They are all deaded," he cried.

I didn't think they were dead the last time I saw them because they were still on the raft. But I also knew it was impossible for Tom to hold Jimmie, Howard, and the rope much longer. And when he finally had to let go from exhaustion, they would all be washed overboard and drowned. Even an excellent swimmer like Tom wouldn't have a chance in the flood. He would be knocked unconscious by an uprooted tree or log. I was sure all three would be drowned as I rode Bess at a gallop into town. I lifted Frankie down from the mare in front of the marshal's office.

"Run and tell Papa what happened," I said.

Then I ran into the marshal's office. Uncle Mark was sitting at his desk.

"Flood on the river!" I shouted. "Tom, Jimmie, and Howard were on the raft!"

Uncle Mark jumped to his feet. "Where?" he asked.

"The last I saw of them was in the rapids!" I cried.

Uncle Mark ran out of the office. His big white stallion, Lightning, was tied to the hitching post. Uncle Mark leaped into the saddle, grabbed my wrist, and lifted me up behind him. We rode at a gallop to the bank of the river just below the rapids. Then Uncle Mark slowed the stallion down as we followed the river downstream.

"They must be drowned!" I cried.

"Stop that bawling and keep your eyes open," Uncle Mark ordered.

About two miles below the rapids there was a sharp curve in the river where it practically reversed the direction in which it was flowing. Uncle Mark pointed.

"There they are!" he said.

The raft had been tossed by the crest of the flood up on the bank of the river. I could see Tom, Jimmie, and Howard lying on the raft, but they weren't moving.

"They're all dead," I cried.

"If they were dead," Uncle Mark said, "they probably wouldn't still be on the raft. But I've got to get them away from that riverbank."

I saw what he meant as I got off Lightning. The force of the floodwater was chewing big chunks out of the riverbank where the raft was. If Uncle Mark didn't reach the raft in time to pull it away from the river, it would fall into the floodwaters. And if that happened, Tom Jimmie, and Howard would be drowned for sure.

I watched Uncle Mark ride Lightning into the floodwaters. I began to pray. Uprooted trees and logs were being hurled with enough force to stun a horse or even kill it. But no wonder Uncle Mark was proud of his stallion.

Lightning swam steadily across the river without balking, although he was nearly hit several times by a log or up-rooted tree before reaching the other side.

The floodwater had carried them about a quarter of a mile downstream. Uncle Mark rode back at a gallop toward the raft. Uncoiling his lariat, he tied one end of it to the pommel of his saddle. I bit my lip in terror as I saw the riverbank cave in under one corner of the raft. Uncle Mark whirled the noose of his lariat over his head and threw it. The loop fell around the oarlock. Uncle Mark slowed Lightning down until the lariat became taut. Then he pulled the raft about fifty feet away from the riverbank. Jumping off Lightning, he ran to the raft. I saw the undermined riverbank where the raft had been suddenly cave in. If Uncle Mark had missed that first throw of the lasso, Tom, Jimmie, and Howard would have dropped into the raging floodwater.

I watched Uncle Mark turn Jimmie over. He put his ear to Jimmie's chest, then to Tom's and Howard's. Then he signaled me and I knew he meant that they were all unconscious but not dead. I watched him carry Jimmie to Lightning and lay him belly down across the saddle. Then he put Howard across Lightning's neck and Tom across the horse's rump. He began slapping all three of them on the back.

I watched Uncle Mark for what seemed like hours but could only have been a few minutes before Papa arrived on a borrowed horse. Several men were with him, including Parley's father, who was carrying some blankets.

"Are they alive?" Papa asked me.

"They must be," Mr. Benson said before I could an-swer, "or the marshal wouldn't be trying to get the water out of them. No sense in all of us getting wet. I've got the whiskey and blankets. I'll go across."

The river was almost as high as when Uncle Mark crossed, but there were no uprooted trees and logs in it now. Mr. Benson swam his horse across and was soon with Uncle Mark.

They carried Jimmie to the raft. Uncle Mark held Jimmie's head up while Mr. Benson forced some whiskey down his throat. I saw Jimmie's head move and then his legs. Then Uncle Mark and Mr. Benson rolled Jimmie in a blanket. I watched them do the same thing with Howard. Then they carried Tom to the raft. I held my breath as they tried to force whiskey down Tom's throat. Tom didn't move. Mr. Benson forced more whiskey into my brother. This time I saw his head move as he struggled unconsciously to avoid the whiskey.

Then I did something that I'd never done before. I fainted.

When I woke up I was home in bed. Frankie was standing by the bed, holding my hand.

"You woked up," he said, smiling. "I'll tell Mamma."

I looked at Tom's bed. It was empty. "Where is Tom?" I asked.

"In Mamma's bed downstairs," Frankie said.

"And Jimmie and Howard?" I asked.

"Nobody is deaded," Frankie said. "They are home in bed."

It wasn't until then that I realized it was morning. I'd slept right through from the time I'd fainted.

"Never mind telling Mamma," I said. "I'm going to get up."

141

"Want to know where Papa went?" he asked as I was getting dressed.

I nodded my head.

"Papa and Uncle Mark took saws and axes to chop up the raft so nobody can ever use it again," Frankie said. "And Papa is real mad at Tom."

"So am I," I said, suddenly feeling an anger against The Great Brain that I had never believed I was capable of feeling.

It was nine o'clock when I went downstairs with Frankie. Mamma and Aunt Bertha were in the kitchen. They both hugged me, as if I'd been away for a long time.

"How do you feel?" Mamma asked.

"Hungry," I answered.

"That is because you haven't had anything to eat since noon yesterday," she said. "I wanted to wake you last night, but Dr. LeRoy said to let you sleep until you woke up by yourself. What would you like for breakfast?"

"Everything," I said. "Mush, hot cakes, bacon and eggs, toast, and milk. Gosh, but I'm hungry. How is Tom?"

"All right, thank God," Mamma said. "You can go talk to him while Bertha and I fix your breakfast."

"I don't care if I never see him again," I said.

Mamma looked at me as if I'd said I was going into her bedroom to cut Tom's throat. "How can you say such a terrible thing about your own brother?" she asked.

"Easy," I said. "How would you feel about somebody who almost killed your two best friends?"

Mamma made me tell her all about it as I ate the biggest breakfast of my life. I told her about Tom swindling me out of my ten percent commission too. She and Papa didn't even know that Tom was charging kids to ride on the raft. But did I get any sympathy? Heck, no.

"Your father and I have warned you time and time again not to make any bets or deals with your brother," she said. "As for what happened to Jimmie Peterson and Howard Kay, your father is going to have a long talk with Tom Dennis. Dr. LeRoy said to keep him in bed until suppertime."

I knew Tom was in for it when Mamma called him by his full name. She only did that when she was very angry.

Eddie Huddle came over to play with Frankie by the time we finished the morning chores. I got my bike and rode over to Jimmie's house. His mother told me I could go up and see him, but he had to remain in bed all day. Jimmie looked pretty darn pale and sick when I entered his room. He propped himself up on a pillow.

"How do you feel?" I asked.

"How would you feel if you'd had a belly and lungs full of muddy river water and almost drowned?" he asked.

"I guess I'd feel pretty bad," I said. "But not as bad as if I'd drowned. Tom did save your life and Howard's."

"Maybe it would have been better if he'd just saved himself and let us drown," Jimmie said to my surprise.

"How do you figure that?" I asked.

"Then all the grownups would hate him, just like the kids do," Jimmie said. "And nobody in town would have anything to do with him and his great brain."

I knew the kids had been avoiding Tom until he built the Explorer and started running excursions on the

143

river. But I sure as heck didn't know they hated my brother.

Jimmie's mother came into the room and said it was time for me to leave. I rode my bike over to Howard's house. His mother said I could see Howard but not to stay too long. Howard was in bed too. He looked pale but not as bad as Jimmie.

"Hello, John," he said in a weak voice.

"How do you feel?" I asked.

"Weak and dizzy," he said.

"You'll get over it," I said. "I'll bet you'll be coming over to play with me by tomorrow."

"I'll never go to your place again until Tom goes away to school," Howard said. "He almost got me drowned just to make thirty cents."

"I begged you and Jimmie not to go," I reminded him.

"Tom made darn sure we had to go," Howard said. "He knew we'd rather go than let the other kids think we were cowards. I never want to speak to him again. But you can come over and play with me any time, John."

"I'm glad you aren't mad at me because Tom is my brother," I said.

"Pa says Tom belongs in a reform school," Howard said. "And Ma wanted to have him arrested for almost getting me drowned. But Pa said no because he is your father's friend."

"I guess I'd better be going now," I said. "Your mother said not to stay too long."

It was lunchtime when Papa returned from helping Uncle Mark destroy the raft. Mamma told him what I'd told her. He made me tell it all over again. And just for good measure, I told him what Jimmie and Howard had said. Usually when Papa got angry, his cheeks would puff up and his face turn red. But the more he listened, the whiter his face became and his cheeks appeared to sink in his face. He looked positively sick by the time I finished.

"I don't know what we are going to do with that boy," he said to Mamma.

I had a few suggestions, like making Tom give me back my dollar and paying me the ten percent commission on the fares he had collected before the wreck of the Explorer. But Papa looked so sad and bewildered that I just kept my mouth shut.

I played with Frankie in the backyard all afternoon. Not one kid came over to play. I knew they weren't swimming because after a flood the water in the river stayed muddy for a couple of days.

Mamma let Tom get up and get dressed late in the afternoon. He came out of the house just as Frankie and I were starting to do the evening chores. We were in the woodshed getting kindling wood when he entered.

"Why haven't you been in to see me?" he asked.

"I told Mamma that I didn't care if I never saw you again," I said. "Papa and Uncle Mark destroyed the raft. That means you swindled me out of my dollar and commission. But that isn't the worst part. You and your money-loving heart almost got my two best friends drowned because you couldn't pass up thirty cents."

"Maybe that last trip was a mistake," he admitted. Then he went over and sat on the railing of the corral fence until it was suppertime.

I sat at the table during supper waiting for Papa to

start blasting Tom, but he didn't. After supper I sat in the parlor waiting for Papa to give Tom a lecture until it was bedtime for Frankie and me. But I knew a blast was coming. I went upstairs with Frankie and took off my shoes.

"You stay here," I said. "I'm going to sneak down the stairway and listen."

I crept down the stairway almost to the bottom. I could hear everything that was said in the parlor.

"If I had known," Papa was saying, "that you were going to charge your friends to ride on the raft, I would never have let you build it. But since you did make them pay, it is only fair and proper that you pay me for using Bess. A team of horses rents for three dollars a day. You will therefore pay me a dollar and a half for each day you used Bess to pull the raft on the stone sled back up the river."

"But that's a lot more money than I made each day," Tom protested.

"What you made," Papa said, "has nothing to do with the going rental price for a team of horses. This morning your Uncle Mark and I destroyed the raft. That means you cannot turn it over to J. D. as promised."

"I didn't destroy the raft," Tom said. "That is J. D.'s hard luck."

"No," Papa said, "that is your hard luck. You will give J. D. back his dollar and pay him the ten percent commission on fares you collected. And we will now get down to the really important part of this raft business."

"Don't you call my having to hand over a fortune important?" Tom asked.

"You," Papa said, "and every boy in this town know

that when it rains hard in the mountains there is a very good possibility of a flood in the river. You knew it had been raining in the mountains all day. You knew the water was turning muddy, indicating the possibility of a flood. And yet you jeopardized the lives of six boys for thirty cents. And as a result, Jimmie Peterson and Howard Kay almost drowned."

"But they didn't drown," Tom protested. "And I risked my own life to save them. Don't I get any credit for that?"

"If you hadn't shamed them into going on the raft with you," Papa said, "there would have been no need for you to risk your life to save them. Now, I've just about had it with you and your great brain. So I am giving you fair warning. If you don't reform, I will send you to the strictest military academy in the United States. So you damn well better reform. Now go to bed."

It was the first time I'd ever heard Papa swear in front of Mamma and Aunt Bertha. I guess that shows how angry he was with Tom. I scooted back upstairs and was starting to undress when Tom entered the room.

"You listened," he said.

"Yes," I said. "And boy, oh, boy, did Papa lay it on you good."

"You told him everything," Tom said with an accusing look. Then he shrugged. "I guess you had to after what happened. And even if you hadn't told him, he would have found out all about it anyway."

"Well?" I asked.

"Well, what?" he said.

"Are you going to reform like Papa said?" I asked.

"Papa is just a little upset," Tom said. "But he will

147

get over it, just as he has in the past. What is the sense in having a great brain if you don't use it?"

"But if you don't reform," I said, "Papa will send you to a military academy."

Tom sat down and took off one shoe. "You sure are dumb when it comes to parents," he said.

"And just how do you figure that?" I asked because no kid likes to be called dumb unless he knows why.

"You didn't hear Mamma say one word, did you?" Tom asked.

"What has that got to do with me being dumb?" I asked.

"Papa told Mamma he was going to lay down the law to me," Tom said. "She knew it was something he had to get off his chest. But Papa knows as well as I do that Mamma would never let him send me away to a military academy. And speaking of academies, I have a proposition for you before I go back to the Catholic Academy in Salt Lake City."

"Not me," I said. "I may be dumb but not dumb enough to make any more deals with you."

"Have it your way," Tom said. "I can sell the basketball and backstop to some other kid before I leave."

That made me change my mind. "What do you want for them?" I asked.

"Let me keep the dollar and ten percent commission money Papa said I had to give you," Tom said, "and you can have the basketball and backstop."

I knew the basketball and backstop cost a lot more than that. And when I owned them, I was a very popular fellow because I didn't charge the kids to play.

"It's a deal," I said.

148

"Shake on it," Tom said.

We shook hands to seal the bargain. I went to bed that night knowing that The Great Brain had no intention of even trying to reform. But in spite of his money-loving heart and the many times he had swindled me, Tom was my brother, and I loved him. The Jesuit priests at the academy had failed to reform him. Papa and Mamma couldn't make him reform. So it was up to me to make Tom turn over a new leaf. I knew I had to do it for his own good.

Tom had taught me to think about a problem before going to sleep and my subconscious mind would solve it. I was thinking very hard of a way to save Tom from himself when I fell asleep.

CHAPTER TEN

The Trial of the Great Brain

THAT TRICK TOM TAUGHT ME of making the subconscious mind solve a problem while you are asleep sure worked. When I woke up in the morning, an idea popped right into my head of a way to make Tom reform. If The Great Brain got a taste of what it would be like to go on trial as a confidence man, swindler, and crook, maybe that would make him reform. I would get the kids to put Tom on trial in our barn.

After the morning chores were over I got my bike and went to Smith's vacant lot. Most of the kids our age were there. I explained my idea to them. They all thought it was a peach of an idea. The only trouble was that all of them wanted to be witnesses against Tom. I couldn't find one kid who wanted to be on the jury. I decided to have Tom tried just by a judge, the way Judge Potter often tried cases in court. But I couldn't find one kid impartial enough to be a judge. They all said Tom was guilty.

Then I happened to look across the street. Harold Vickers was sitting on his front porch, reading a book. Harold was always reading. He was the son of the district attorney and sixteen years old. He had something the matter with his eyes and wore glasses with thick lenses. I walked over to the front porch, explained everything to Harold, and asked him to be the judge.

"You've come to the right person," he said, looking at me over his glasses. "I am going to be a lawyer when I grow up. That's why I spend most of my time reading about the law, or in court listening to my father try cases. It will be a pleasure to act as judge and put that smart aleck brother of yours in his place."

I didn't think what Harold said was prejudiced because he had never been swindled himself by The Great Brain. And Harold agreed that making myself district attorney wasn't prejudiced either. Even though he was my brother, Tom had swindled me more times than any kid in town. That made me impartial.

It was lunchtime when I got home. I was pretty darn sure every kid in town my age and Tom's knew about the trial. After eating, I sneaked some evidence I would need into the barn without Tom seeing me. Then I joined Tom, who was playing basketball by himself.

"I thought there would be a gang of kids here to play basketball," he said, "now that they don't have to pay to play."

151

"They will all be in our barn at two o'clock," I said.

"What's going on?" he asked.

"You are," I said. "You are going on trial for being a swindler, confidence man, crook, and anything else we can think of."

"What kind of a joke is this?" he asked, laughing.

"It is no joke," I said. "And if you want to try to defend yourself, you be in the barn at two o'clock."

Harold Vickers came at one thirty, as promised. He helped me move bales of hay inside the barn to make a bench for the judge, a witness stand, and a place for the district attorney and defendant to sit. There were about forty kids in the barn before two o'clock. Tom was still playing basketball by himself in the alley. I went to the barn door and opened it.

"Hear ye, hear ye!" I shouted. "Court is about to begin!"

I saw Tom put the basketball in the woodshed and start for the barn. I knew his curiosity would make him come.

"What's going on here?" he demanded.

Harold picked up Papa's wooden mallet. He rapped it on a block of wood we had placed on the bale of hay serving as the judge's bench.

"Silence in the court," Harold ordered. "This court is now in session. The Honorable Judge Harold Vickers presiding." Harold had spent so much time in court that he sounded like a real judge.

I stood up. "I call the first case, Your Honor," I said. "The kids of Adenville against Tom Fitzgerald, alias The Great Brain."

Harold looked at Tom over his thick glasses. "Does

the defendant have an attorney?" he asked.

"I'll defend myself," Tom said smugly.

"You are charged," Harold said, "with being a confidence man, a swindler, a crook, and a blackmailer, and with the attempted murder of Jimmie Peterson and Howard Kay. How do you plead?"

"Not guilty," Tom said confidently.

I could tell from the look on Tom's face that he had decided to play along with the trial, believing his great brain would make fools out of all of us.

Harold pointed the mallet at me. "Call your first witness, Mr. District Attorney," he said.

Tom held up his hand. "Just a minute, Your Honor," he said. "I demand a jury trial."

This time Harold pointed the mallet at Tom. "How can you have a jury trial when every kid in town is against you?" he asked. "Now sit down and shut up or I'll fine you for contempt of court."

I called Danny Forester as my first witness. I made him place his hand on an old Bible and swear to tell the truth.

"Now, Danny," I said, "tell the judge what happened to you after the defendant swindled you out of your infielder's glove."

Tom jumped up. "I object, Your Honor," he said. "Danny made a bet with me and lost. There is no law against betting in Utah."

I had expected this. I got seven tin cans from where I'd hidden them and placed them on a bale of hay. I then explained to Harold how Tom had swindled Danny and Jimmie.

"And if that isn't a swindle, Your Honor," I said as

I finished, "I don't know what you would call it."

"The court rules," Harold said, "that it was an out-and-out swindle. Proceed."

"Now, Danny," I said, "tell the judge what happened afterward."

"My Pa gave me the worst whipping of my life," Danny said. "And he told me that I could never have another baseball glove."

"Cross-examine," I said to Tom.

Tom walked confidently to the witness stand. "When you made the bet, Danny," he said, "you thought you were going to win two dollars and a quarter from me, didn't you?"

"I guess so," Danny answered.

"And, after seeing four other kids win twenty-five cents from me," Tom said, "you thought you had a sure thing, didn't you?"

"I guess so," Danny said, looking almost ashamed.

"In other words," Tom said, "you thought you had a sure thing and I thought I had a sure thing. So how can you say I swindled you without admitting that you tried to swindle me?"

Danny gave me a helpless look. I didn't know what to do so I passed on the helpless look to the judge. Harold pointed the wooden mallet at me.

"I would like to point out to the district attorney," he said, "a flaw in the defendant's line of reasoning. The witness only *thought* that he had a sure thing. The defendant *knew* that he had a sure thing. So the court rules the witness was swindled. Call the next witness."

Boy, oh, boy, was I glad I'd picked Harold for the

judge. I called Jimmie Peterson to the witness stand and put him under oath.

"Now, Jimmie," I said, "tell the judge what happened to you after the defendant swindled you out of your baseball with the same confidence trick."

"My ma gave me a whipping," Jimmie said, "and told me that I could never have another baseball because I'd let that Fitzgerald kid cheat me out of mine."

"Now, Jimmie," I said, "tell the judge why you got on that raft for the last trip, when you knew there was a flood coming down the river."

Again Tom stood up. "I object, Your Honor," he said. "The witness couldn't possibly have known there was a flood coming down the river. The water in the river has turned muddy many times before without there being any flood."

Harold looked at me. I just stared back at him because I didn't know what to say. Then he peered over his glasses at Tom.

"You are right about the water in the river becoming muddy without there being a flood," he said. "But this has only happened when it was raining in and close around Adenville and not in the mountains. Every time it rains all day or all night in the mountains and the water in the river starts turning muddy, there has been a flood. So the court rules that when he saw the muddy water on that day, he knew a flood was coming down the river."

Boy, oh, boy, Harold was turning out to be as smart when it came to law as his father.

"Now, Jimmie," I said. "Answer the question."

Jimmie pointed at Tom. "I got on the raft," he said,

"because Tom said anybody who didn't go was a fraidy-cat. And I didn't want the other kids to think I was a coward."

"Cross-examine," I said to Tom.

The Great Brain stared at Jimmie. "Is this the thanks I get for saving your life?" he asked.

"You wouldn't have had to save it," Jimmie said, "if you hadn't shamed me into going on the raft."

Tom walked back and sat down on a bale of hay. For once in his life a kid had stunned him into silence. I called Howard Kay as my next witness.

"Now, Howard," I said, after swearing him in, "tell the judge why you went on that last trip on the raft."

"Same reason as Jimmie," he said. "I didn't want the kids to think I was a fraidy-cat."

"Then the defendant actually forced you to go," I said.

"He sure did," Howard said.

"In other words," I said, "Tom Fitzgerald, alias The Great Brain, is guilty of attempting to drown you and Jimmie."

"I object!" Tom shouted. "Howard knows that I couldn't attempt to drown him and Jimmie."

Harold pointed the wooden mallet at Tom. "You used words which forced both the witnesses to get on the raft," he said, "which is the same as if you had used physical force, in the eyes of the law. The court rules that because you didn't cancel that last trip, you are guilty of the attempted murder of Howard Kay and Jimmie Peterson. Proceed, Mr. District Attorney."

There wasn't a doubt in my mind by this time that

156

Harold Vickers would one day be a member of the Supreme Court of the United States.

"One last question, Howard," I said. "Are you willing to forgive the defendant?"

"Shucks, no," Howard said. "I hate him."

"Cross-examine," I said to Tom.

I'd never seen such a bewildered look on Tom's face as he walked to the witness stand.

"Do you really hate me, Howard?" he asked.

"You sure as heck haven't given me any reason to like you," Howard answered.

I couldn't help feeling sorry for Tom as he slumped down on a bale of hay. But I couldn't stop now. It was up to me to make Tom reform—no matter how much it hurt me or him. I called Parley Benson to the stand. I didn't know if I should ask him to take off his coonskin cap in court or not. I decided to let him wear it.

"Now, Parley," I said, "please tell the judge how you lost your King air rifle."

"Tom said he had a piece of magnetic wood," Parley said. "He claimed he could throw it into the air and make it come back to him, using a magnet. I knew nobody could magnetize wood and that's why I bet him."

I brought out Papa's big dictionary and opened it to the page with a picture of a boomerang. I showed the picture to Parley.

"Is that what the piece of wood looked like?" I asked.

Parley stared at the picture. "Yeah," he said. "That looks just like it."

"Your Honor," I said, "according to this dictionary, this is a picture of a boomerang, which is described as a

157

bent or curved piece of wood originally used by the aborigines of Australia. By shaping the piece of wood a certain
way, it can be thrown and will return to the person who
threw it."

"Let me see that," Harold said.

I gave him the dictionary and then turned to Parley.
"Now, Parley," I said, "if you had known the piece of
wood was a boomerang, would you have bet?"

"Shucks, no," Parley said.

"What happened because you lost the air rifle?" I
asked.

"My pa horsewhipped me," Parley said. "But that
wasn't the worst part. Pa had promised me a twenty-two
rifle when I was fifteen. But he said that if I couldn't take
care of an air rifle then I couldn't take care of a twenty-
two. I guess I'll be lucky if Pa ever lets me have a real
rifle now."

"Cross-examine," I said to Tom.

The Great Brain walked to the witness stand. "You
are under oath to tell the truth," he said. "Now, isn't it a
fact that you thought I'd gone crazy when you made the
bet?"

"Well, yeah," Parley admitted.

"And isn't it a fact that you thought you were taking
advantage of an insane person to win two dollars?" Tom
asked.

Parley looked helplessly at me as if he expected me to
answer the question. I sure as heck didn't know how to
answer it without making Parley guilty and Tom not
guilty. But Harold did.

"The defendant is confusing the issue," Harold said.
"The court rules that the defendant pretended to have a

magnetic stick and feigned insanity for the sole purpose of swindling the witness. Call your next witness, Mr. District Attorney."

Boy, oh, boy, if I hadn't picked Harold for a judge, Tom would have been found not guilty on all charges. I called several more witnesses who had been swindled by Tom. The Great Brain didn't cross-examine any of them. I saved Frankie for my last witness.

"Now, Frankie," I said. "Tell the judge how Tom tried to make a blackmailer out of you."

"Tom made you give him your basketball and backstop," Frankie said, "for not telling Papa and Mamma you said he wasn't a Christian. He told me to make you give me something for not telling. I made you give me your jackknife. Then you called Tom and me blackmailers. I didn't know what it meant until I asked Papa. He told me a blackmailer was one of the most low-down crooks there is. I didn't want to be a low-down crook so I gave you back your jackknife."

"Now tell the judge," I said, "how Tom played a low-down joke on you and made you run away from home."

"I didn't want to run away," Frankie said. "But when you and Tom didn't try to stop me, I was sure Papa and Mamma didn't love me anymore. So I runned away."

I was sorry I'd asked the question. I wanted Frankie to put all the blame on Tom. I thought for sure Tom would cross-examine to let everybody know it was as much my fault as his fault that Frankie had run away. But he just sat there staring at Frankie and shook his head when I said, "Cross-examine."

"Your Honor," I said, after excusing Frankie from the witness stand, "the prosecution has proved that Tom

Fitzgerald, alias The Great Brain, is a confidence man, a swindler, a crook, and a blackmailer with such a money-loving heart that he almost killed two boys for thirty cents. He is doomed to become a desperate criminal who will end up at the end of a hangman's rope some day if he doesn't reform. I'm finished now. What do I say?"

"You say 'The state rests,' " Harold told me.

"The state rests, Your Honor," I said, and sat down on the bale of hay.

Harold looked at Tom. "The defense will now present its case," he said.

Tom moved slowly to the witness stand. "I have only one witness for the defense," he said. "Myself." He raised his right hand and placed his left hand on the Bible. "I swear to tell the truth, the whole truth, and nothing but the truth, so help me God."

Tom looked at the faces of all the kids, then at Harold and me. Then he said slowly, "When this trial started, I thought it was a big joke and that my great brain would make you all look like fools. Instead, for the first time in my life, I see myself as others see me."

Harold peered over his glasses. "Are you trying to tell this court that you didn't know you were a confidence man, a swindler, a crook, and a blackmailer?" he asked.

"I didn't consider myself any of those things," Tom said. "I just thought I was using my great brain to outsmart other kids and adults. I didn't know Danny, Jimmie, and Parley had gotten a whipping for losing those things. I didn't know that Danny could never have another baseball glove, and Jimmie could never have another baseball, and Parley could never have a twenty-two rifle. They never mentioned it to me. I didn't know Frankie

160

thought I was trying to make a blackmailer out of him. I believed all the fellows liked me and were my friends."

Harold shook his head. "Just because you say you didn't know all these things is no excuse," he said.

"I am not asking to be excused," Tom said. "I am only asking to be allowed to make amends for some of the things I have done. I promise to return the baseball glove to Danny and the baseball to Jimmie and the air rifle to Parley. And I ask the court for leniency."

Harold stared at Tom. "Why should the court give a confessed confidence man, swindler, crook, and blackmailer like you any leniency?" he demanded.

"Because I believe the good I have done with my great brain should be judged also," Tom said. "I saved the fathers of most of the kids here from losing money in the Alkali Flats swindle. Danny's father would have lost enough money to buy a hundred infielder's gloves. Jimmie's mother would have lost enough money to buy a hundred baseballs. Parley's father, enough money to buy a hundred King air rifles. And no matter how or why Jimmie and Howard got on the raft, the fact remains that I did risk my life to save theirs. And if it hadn't been for me, the kids in this town would never have known the joy of sailing a raft on the river. The defense rests, Your Honor."

"Leave the barn, I mean the court, now," Harold said. "The defendant can't be in court while his fate is being decided."

Tom walked out of the barn with a slump in his shoulders.

Harold looked at me. "Does the district attorney believe the defendant will reform?" he asked.

161

"It wasn't Tom's great brain that made him a confidence man, swindler, crook, and blackmailer," I said, "but his money-loving heart. They say for a person to reform they must have a change of heart. And for my money, it will break Tom's money-loving heart to give all those things back. Can't you give him another chance?"

"I can give him a suspended sentence," Harold said, "as soon as we decide what the sentence is to be."

"It was my idea," I said, "that if Tom refused to reform none of the kids in town would play with him, or speak to him, or have anything to do with him until he does reform."

Harold looked around the barn. "If I suspend the sentence," he said, "how many of you kids will be Tom's friend?"

Parley was the first to speak. "Seeing as how I'm getting my air rifle back," he said, "I'll be his friend."

"Same here," Danny said.

"Me too," Jimmie said.

Harold peered over his glasses at the rest of the kids. "If I suspend the sentence," he said, "it means you all have to be Tom's friend for as long as he stays reformed. How many are in favor of a suspended sentence?"

All the kids except Howard Kay held up their hands. Then Howard slowly raised his right hand.

"Bring the defendant back," Harold ordered.

I sent Frankie for Tom. When they entered the barn, The Great Brain was holding Frankie's hand as if he wanted someone to hang on to. He didn't let go as he stood before the judge.

"Tom Fitzgerald, alias The Great Brain," Harold said, "you have been found guilty on all charges. Have you

anything to say before sentence is passed on you?"

"I promise to reform and never use my great brain to swindle or hurt anybody again," Tom said.

"It is the sentence of this court," Harold said, "that no boy in Adenville will play with you or speak to you or have anything to do with you for one year."

I could see Tom was shocked because he staggered backwards a step.

"However," Harold said, "due to the fact that you have promised to reform, I hereby suspend the sentence. But if you pull one crooked stunt during the year, I will revoke the suspended sentence." Harold hit the block of wood with the wooden mallet. "This court is adjourned," he said.

Then a sort of strange thing happened. Harold came down from the bench and shook hands with Tom. Then all the kids crowded around The Great Brain to shake hands and pat him on the back. At first I thought it was because they wanted to show they had no hard feelings. But after thinking it over, I saw there was another reason. They knew they didn't have to worry about The Great Brain swindling them anymore.

By suppertime everybody in town knew that The Great Brain had promised to reform. Papa tried to take all the credit. He said it was his threat to send Tom to a military academy that did it. Mamma didn't let him get away with taking all the credit. She said it was her prayers to St. Jude that did it. But all the kids in town knew it was the trial that had brought about The Great Brain's reformation.

I thought for sure Mayor Whitlock would declare a town holiday, and that Papa would get out an extra of the *Adenville Weekly Gazette* with a headline reading: THE GREAT BRAIN REFORMS. But neither of these things happened. What did happen was that people congratulated Papa as if he was the father of a new baby. And some women who hadn't spoken to Mamma for months now became her friends again.

I'm telling you, the way people acted you would think Tom had just paid off the debts of all the adults in town and reduced the school year to thirty days. Grownups and kids stopped him on the street to shake his hand. It was as if he had become a hero by promising to reform.

But I have to end this book with a confession. Remember that brilliant plea I made to the judge to give Tom another chance? I had my fingers crossed all the time I was making it. I was the only person in Adenville who had any doubts that The Great Brain was really going to reform. For my money, a fox clever enough to get into a chicken coop doesn't stop stealing chickens just because the rooster starts crowing and the hens start cackling. If I was right, it would make me the smartest kid in town. But I hoped I was wrong, even if it made me the dumbest kid in town.

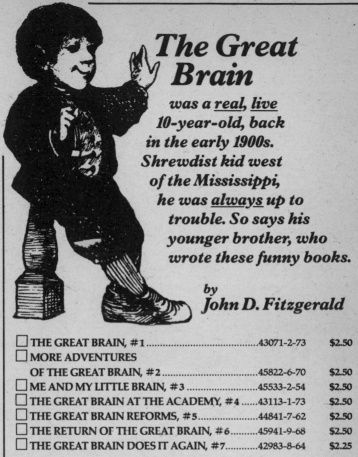